# THE STONE BOYS

Selected Previous Works

Fiction

*An American Mystic*
*The Miracle*
*The Odyssey of Telemachus*
*The Blind Woman*

Nonfiction

*The Wonder of Boys*
*The Wonder of Girls*
*Boys and Girls Learn Differently*
*Saving Our Sons*
*The Minds of Girls*
*The Wonder of Aging*
*The Soul of the Child*

Poetry

*Emptying*
*The Sabbath*
*Ancient Wisdom, Modern Words*
*As the Swans Gather*

# MICHAEL GURIAN

This book contains sensitive material.
Parental guidance recommended.

LATAH
BOOKS

SPOKANE, WASHINGTON

For permissions contact: editor@latahbooks.com
This book is a work of fiction. Any references to historical events, real
people, or real places are used fictitiously. Other names, characters, places,
and events are products of the author's imagination, and any resemblance to
actual events or places or persons, living or dead, is entirely coincidental.

ISBN: 978-0-9997075-7-9

Cataloging-in-Publication Data is available upon request
Manufactured in the United States of America

Cover design by Marina Gulova

Book design by Gray Dog Press
www.graydogpress.com

Published by
Latah Books, Spokane, Washington
www.latahbooks.com

The author may be contacted at:
michaelgurian@comcast.net

This book may be purchased in bulk for educational purposes.
For bulk orders please email: editor@latahbooks.com

# DEDICATION

For my family, Gail, Gabrielle, and Davita

And for all the invisible boys

# FOREWORD

When Michael asked me to introduce his novel, I was honored and glad to do so. Michael and I met nearly forty years ago when we were working on our Masters in Fine Arts at Eastern Washington University. Before the publication of my first novel, *Stuck in Neutral,* I co-authored two books with Michael in the Parenting, Psychology and Education fields: *Boys and Girls Learn Differently* and *What Stories Does My Son Need?* While Michael is best known for his non-fiction work in these fields, many people don't know that he is also a talented novelist and poet. *The Stone Boys* is his first young adult novel. Michael is a sexual abuse survivor, and the power of this story grows from his own experiences as a boy.

Michael started sketching this story out when he was 18, just after he told his parents about his abuse at 10 years old. Over the next two decades he worked on *The Stone Boys* and then shelved it as he and his wife, Gail, raised their daughters and Michael published bestselling nonfiction books like *The Wonder of Boys* and *The Wonder of Girls.*

In the late 1990s, soon after publishing *Boys and Girls Learn Differently,* Michael showed several agents his latest version of *The Stone Boys.* Because he was established as a family counselor and nonfiction writer, these folks told him to hold off publishing this novel.

"There's sexuality in this," they said. "There's some very painful stuff here."

So, he put down the project again.

One day at lunch recently, I asked him about *The Stone Boys* and Michael admitted he was still working on it. I urged him to finally get it published.

"You're turning 60 this year," I reminded him. "This book should be part of your legacy. It is important. Finish this book and get it out there!"

Michael sat back, pondering.

"I'm going to publish it," he told me a few days later, and I was glad. While a part of me wishes he hadn't waited so long, this newest version, a very powerful young adult novel, is well worth the wait.

Nonfiction traps us in facts and the search for them. There are great possibilities in true stories, but fiction gives us the freedom to tell truths that go deeper into visions and understandings of spiritual and personal reality—and especially into emotional truths.

The two boys in this novel are every boy or girl who has struggled with abuse, trauma, loss, pain, good and evil, and the quest for truth and justice—and like all great stories, the universality comes from the specificity of the characters' lives and struggles.

The narrator, a 17-year-old boy, expresses his inner world fearlessly. Some people never find the courage. I can think of no one better than Michael Gurian to write this story and I hope you will let yourself *feel* it as much as I have.

Terry Trueman
Printz Honor Award Winner for *Stuck in Neutral*

# THE STONE BOYS

# PROLOGUE

*June 15, 1975*

SIXTEEN YEARS OLD and dressed in a long sleeve plaid shirt, blue jeans and blue sneakers, Dave McConnell walked through the forest that bordered Vallecito Lake in southwest Colorado. He had hitchhiked up to the lake's south boat entrance from Durango and was making his way by foot through a forest that smelled of honeysuckle and mulch. He spotted a nest in the crotch of two elm branches, and a sparrow dove at him, warning him to stay away. Swatting at the sparrow defensively, he kept moving through thick undergrowth to the place where he had stacked fir branches into piles a couple months ago. Nothing had changed in the makeshift wall. His secret world was safe. He struggled on through thick trees and bushes until he came to his private lagoon, kept hidden from the lake by a rock wall.

Walking onto the sand, thinking his usual million thoughts, he found his spot on the fallen tree, its bark worn down by his butt. He set his fishing pole, canteen, book, and sandwich down on the bark next to him and pulled his plaid shirt over his shoulders. The sun hit his pale arms, and he frowned at the ugly zits and blackheads on his upper chest, upper arms and, though he couldn't see them now, his neck and face. Digging into his Campbell's soup can, he pulled out an oozing night crawler, ran his fish hook through it, and cast his line. Once the red and white bobber hit the water, he set the rod to ballast in the crook of his crossed legs and opened his favorite book, Isaac Asimov's *Foundation*, where he joined the Grandmaster and the planets and the stars.

He'd just turned a page when he saw his bobber jumping. He quickly put his book down and reeled in a small sunfish, its tiny mouth opening and closing like a machine. Inside the lining of slimy gills, the tiny hook shined in sunlight. Dave pulled it out, tearing some of the gill in the process. The fish's slime and panic made holding difficult, but Dave held it in his hands for so long he knew the fish teetered just this side of death. More than once he had watched fish die in his hands.

This time, he saved the fish's life by throwing it into the water just in time. Wiping his hands together to remove the slime, he watched the fish freeze perfectly still under water, then suddenly dart away. Dave walked to the water's edge to wash his hands and realized he was baking in the sun. He moved back to his seat, ate his baloney sandwich, and then tugged off his sneakers and socks. He stopped to listen, and hearing no one, stepped out of his jeans, folded them onto the log, and touched his underwear.

Whenever he came here, he debated whether he should take his jockey shorts off. On the one hand, he felt terrified that someone would come and see his naked, hairless, acne-covered pale body. On the other hand, he hated wearing clammy underwear all the way back home after a swim. For months he had seen no one here, so he chose nakedness. Sliding his index fingers along each hip, he pushed his jockey shorts down under his feet, swished sand out of them, and set them on his jeans. Naked now, he walked out into the lagoon a few feet until the cool water stung his genitals. He gasped from the cold but continued downward until his body was acclimated. In a minor act of rebellion against his mother ("Don't swim until a half hour after you eat"), he swam out toward the jutting rocks, and then lay floating on his stomach. He yelled loudly under water, his muffled voice sounding to him as if he yelled in outer space.

"Davey!"

Shocked by the call of his own name, he looked up, wiped his eyes, and saw an empty shore.

"Davey!"

Shivering and frightened, he looked again and saw Allen Tremmel coming out of the forest onto the beach. On his left side were two other seniors, Stu Horst and a Hispanic guy Dave thought was named Carlos Hernandez. Allen wore his usual cowboy shirt with pearl buttons and a blue swim suit with a stripe down each hip. Stu and Carlos were shirtless, their t-shirts hanging from the back of their brown shorts. Stu's chest was white and freckled with some red hair. Carlos was wiry, browner skinned, with a big black mole above his left nipple.

"Hey little Davey Crackers, we could've given you a ride," Allen grinned. "You didn't have to hitchhike."

Allen's presence in this haven was the worst possible thing. Allen was a sick, mean bully. He had thrown Dave into the snow after gym class without his clothes more than once and had locked him out so that everyone saw little Davey naked and crying. Afterwards, the principal, Mr. Jenkins, gave Allen ten swats with the board, but that just made Allen beat Dave up even more. This last February, Allen and four other guys, including Stu, held Dave down spread-eagle naked on the wooden bench in the locker room after gym class and used a razor to scrape along Dave's private parts. "Still no hair!" Allen had laughed, showing everyone what a late bloomer Dave McConnell was—almost six feet tall but no hair anywhere.

Dave watched Allen and the other boys approach and cried, "Go away!"

Allen lifted his sunglasses up onto his head of crew cut hair. "Go away," he imitated, making it sound like a little girl or an old grandma.

Stu opened Isaac Asimov's book and read aloud, "From the library of David McConnell."

Dave turned to look to the lake for rescue and saw boats far off behind the mouth of the lagoon. *What if I scream? Would they hear?* Dave turned back toward Allen, hating how blank his mind was. *I have no plan. I need a plan.*

"Allen, don't . . . do anything," he heard himself whine. "Please." Whining was the worst thing, a self-protective instinct he seemed unable to grow out of.

Allen imitated him again with the little girl voice. "Allen, don't do anything. Please, please." Grabbing *Foundation* from Stu's hands, Allen yanked on each side, broke the book's spine, and tossed it out into the water like a Frisbee.

"No!" Dave shouted. He rushed toward the book and got there in time to lift it with both hands above his head like the soldiers with rifles he'd seen on TV fording rivers in Vietnam.

Allen and the others stalked after him with their arms out as if they were all one person or animal, their faces grinning and concentrating. Dave spun around frantically, pummeling the water as he tried swimming away. Hands grabbed him by his long blond hair, pulled his head underwater, and dragged him screaming, choking, gasping to the sandy shore. Dave was thrown face first into the sand, a knee pushed into his spine. As he sucked in air, barely able to see through water-filled eyes, he felt his jockey shorts shoved into his mouth.

"Stu, give me those shoe laces," Allen commanded.

"I'm sorry," Dave muffled through the shorts. "Please don't hurt me. Please go away."

"Okay, now turn him over," Allen directed.

The boys turned him, and Dave lay spread-eagle on his back like the times in the locker room. His body was no longer his own but Allen's to control, his pale hairless skin shining white in the sun as Stu and Carlos held him tight at the wrists and ankles. Allen tried to tie the shoelace to Dave's scrotum but he spasmed and Allen slapped Dave on the stomach. The soft blow gave Dave hope. He struggled again, but Allen punched him in the stomach much harder this time and Dave screamed so hard the gag blew out of his mouth.

"Brave little guy," Allen laughed. He pushed Dave's jockey shorts back into his mouth, then punched him in the nuts.

Dave's body convulsed, knife-pain shooting through his torso, a pain so terrible nothing compared to it—not belt-whipping discipline from his father, not the broken arm when he was little and fell off a swing, nothing. Dave screamed and struggled so much Stu said, "Take it easy, Allen," but Allen punched Dave in the stomach again. Dave's eyes filled with tears. He felt Carlos let go of his left ankle and kicked. Carlos grabbed the leg again, shoving it down hard.

"Turn him, boys," Allen instructed.

As he was turned, sand scratched Dave's side and face and stomach and genitals and he flew into outer space, to the spaceship where he was a little boy at a piano seated next to a tall teacher who showed him how to use the piano as the spaceship's phaser gun—a big version of a gun Mr. Spock or Captain Kirk would use. Dave now fired blue laser beams at Allen and the boys, evaporating them as Dave felt the tip of his fishing pole push into his right buttock. As Dave struggled in spasms of strength that were not enough to unlock his body from the bigger boys' hands, he lasered them again and again, yet felt the fishing pole covered with rough sand pushing at the opening of his rectum. Dave struggled and screamed into the gag. Allen couldn't get the pole in very deep, but still it hurt it hurt it hurt.

"Allen, look!" Stu said as he released Dave's right wrist.

"Oh man!" Allen shouted. "We gotta get out of here."

Dave watched their hairy legs run across the beach and into the forest. When they were gone, he pulled his underwear out of his mouth, jumped up, ran into the water and rubbed at his anus. He looked toward the shore, saw the fishing pole and seemed to feel it inside him still. Beyond the lagoon he heard the happy screams of a water skier as the boat came towards the rock before veering off and trailing its inevitable white wake behind it.

Dave waited, shivering in the water, unsure what to do next except to get control of his tears. Were Allen and the others waiting for him in the trees? Probably not, he guessed, his sobs subsiding. The boat was gone, but the boys hadn't reappeared.

Dave moved toward the shore through the heavy water. He put his clothes back on and then walked back toward the road, his wet clothes heavy on his body, his shoes sloshing with every step. At the top of a densely wooded rise, he paused for a moment, breathing heavily, carefully watching all around him. "I will never be able to come here again," he said aloud, remembering his hair being pulled by Allen and Stu, the boys' hands grabbing each strand of it to drag him to the sandy beach. Vomit rose, and he poured his lunch onto the trunk of a fir tree. He dropped to his knees and could not stop rib-wrenching waves of puke and then heaves of yellow bile. When the panic and shame finally ended, he stood up, brushed his knees, and tried to spit out the taste of bile.

"I'm gonna get you, Allen," he hollered, his voice shameful to him for its squeaking.

And then an elegant plan began to form. He could get revenge. He would need patience, but it could work perfectly.

His thoughts were absolutely right and moral and good, he was sure of it.

# CHAPTER 1

MY DAD PICKED ME UP from the Durango airport on a hot summer day. Earlier that morning, I'd flown in a big 737 from New York City to Denver and then hopped on a tiny six-seat Cessna propeller plane to this mountain town. Durango was at such a high altitude that I was light-headed and felt like I had to pant to breathe.

"You'll get used to it," Harvey promised me as he turned his rattling, light blue Dodge Dart into the driveway of a dilapidated house halfway down a cul-de-sac called Folsom Place. His lawn was brown, mowed but not edged, and weeds grew where there should have been flowers. Bits of beige paint peeled from the shutters, and there were spots of dried moss on the roof shingles.

"This house of yours needs some help," I critiqued as I opened the car door and studied the place. On the wide front porch, in front of a big bay living room window, a rattan swinging chair sat empty, touched just slightly by a cooling breeze.

"That's why *you're* here," Harvey quipped. "Indentured servitude."

"Sure," I said, turning away, a bit irritated by him already even though I did like him.

Harvey was a pretty good playwright. This year, he was making a small living from a National Endowment for the Humanities grant on the nearby reservation where he would develop and direct the first traveling Native American repertoire theater in the U.S. Harvey seemed content to get away from my mom and New York and eke out a living doing what he loved. My mom, a psychologist and professor at NYU, made good money. She and Harvey got along well enough, as long as they lived miles apart. Harvey said they got divorced because she wanted to "find herself" without him holding her back. She said it was more complicated.

The Dodge Dart was still sputtering as I pulled my big brown traveling trunk out of the back seat of the car. Too heavy for me alone, Harvey helped push it to the asphalt and then came over to grip the other handle and steer it toward the house.

"Make this your home, son," Harvey said as he guided me through a brown living room with a big brown couch and chair, past the dining room table covered with papers and books and a typewriter. In the kitchen the floor creaked with every step, and we dropped the trunk on the floor. Harvey opened the fridge for something cool to drink as I appraised the faded gold decor—refrigerator, countertops, cupboards, pantry door, even the curtains, gold.

"It's precious, isn't it?" Harvey opened his arms wide. "I wouldn't change a thing!"

He couldn't anyway, since this was a rental, but I knew how his brain worked and laughed at the irony of him being financially broke, as always, but living in a house made of gold.

"Yeah," I agreed, taking a bottle of Coke from him.

"It's so good to see you, son!" he beamed, flipping the cap off a Schlitz beer bottle.

"I guess this town'll be cool," I managed.

"Good, good."

Sitting down on two wooden stools against the kitchen counter, we got caught up on stuff about Mom, New York, what classes I would take in my senior year. "You've grown so much," he said, following it up with other dad sentiments.

Harvey, at 5' 8", had been shorter than me for a couple years (I got my height from my mom's side of the family). He had a graying goatee and long black hair pulled back tight in a rubber-band. He seemed much older to me this summer than last, with new gray streaks like long seams going down from the top of his head into his ponytail. He still wore his "Harvey uniform" of blue jeans, short sleeve white shirt and vest. He owned three vests—a brown leather one, a white one with flower designs on it, and his favorite, a vest of about ten different vertical stripes of color, which he wore today, to celebrate my coming. His neck looked rooster-like, and the skin on his face had lines all over it. Even his hairy arms under the short sleeves had more wrinkles than last summer.

"I'll check Durango out all the way," I promised.

"And check Dave McConnell out." For the last few weeks on the phone he had told me about this kid, a potential friend. "He just lives two doors down. Right there—" he pointed to the blue and white house with blue shutters and a well-tended garden. "He's extremely bright, only about a year younger than you. He wants to be a writer, he likes to play chess and foosball, the family's Catholic but he has Jewish connections back to New York through his mom. I guess he used to be a piano prodigy when he was little, so he likes music like you, Ben. It's a meant-to-be friendship, I just know it. If you do become friends, you're welcome to bring him out to the Rez with us whenever you want, and you can make the basement of this house all your own private place."

"Sure," I said. "Whatever."

He seemed relieved, or just already moving on to a new thought as he bent to pull off his brown loafers and massage his feet. I took a long cold drink of the Coke and knew what we were really talking about. We would get along well enough during the summer after a few days of me being morose and angry and missing my mom and my friend Jeremy and my other friends in New York. After that, Harvey and I would spend "quality time" together at this house, around town, and at the "Rez," but I would need to find my own life too. This meant finding a good friend to help fight my usual summer loneliness.

"I used to walk in the scrublands a lot when I first got here," he said, pointing in their direction through the kitchen window. "That acreage is huge. I see Dave go out there sometimes. Maybe you can go out there with him. The place could be like Sherwood Forest for you boys."

Though I had grown out of Robin Hood, I nodded and said, "Sure." He grinned again, knowing he was pushing too hard as he bent again to rub his feet. Glancing at a slightly balding spot at the top of his head, I pictured him walking the dirt trails, looking for inspiration, an artistic guy who worked way too hard and just didn't succeed like my mom.

"Let me show you the basement," he offered.

"We'll be okay," I reassured my father, descending the stairs with him. "Everything will be fine."

He said he was sure it would and showed me a big open space with lots of stuff stored everywhere. The next morning, while Harvey was at work, I put on my jean shorts and Led Zeppelin t-shirt and began turning the basement into my summer hangout spot. First, I moved Harvey's mannequins and props and boxes of books into corners. Then I pulled the basement couch, card table, and foosball table where I wanted them. I cleaned up the record player and speakers so they worked. I took a chessboard and chess pieces from Harvey's boxes, placed them onto an old card table, and faced two chairs toward each other on opposite sides of the board. I taped my Pac Man and Asteroid posters to the concrete walls and pulled my favorite record albums, books, and comic books from my trunk.

There were two empty shelves on the south wall, so I stood the albums up between two bookends and began arranging Hermann

Hesse's *Siddhartha*, Carlos Castaneda's *Teachings of Don Juan*, Lao Tzu's *Tao Te Ching*, and twenty other books there.

When I got my books and albums just right, I went upstairs to my backpack in my bedroom and got my valuables (Playboys, Penthouses, marijuana) and hid them downstairs behind my record albums, against the concrete wall. I had been getting stoned since I was fourteen. My stomach got queasy just about every day and pot helped my stomach feel good. Lots of things made me feel sick. Sometimes, a bad memory would come into my head, or I would meet a new person and try to be friends, or I wouldn't do something right for my mom and make her sad, or I would rebel against her by doing something crazy, or I would mess up a test and say something mean to someone. My worst times of nausea were the first few weeks before and after visiting my father in whichever new place he was living. Just yesterday I puked at the airport, bent over a toilet bowl in a dirty bathroom stall, wishing I could get stoned. My mother kept trying to get me to stop, but my father didn't get in the way, as if he understood why I needed it, or just wanted to be my friend.

After I finished the basement I came back upstairs, and Harvey suggested I go meet Dave McConnell or some of the other neighbors. We walked around meeting our neighbors, Mr. and Mrs. Filmont, both of whom wore Stetson hats while gardening, the Hutsinpillers across the street, who had three children, and lots of others. The McConnells, though, weren't home. In fact, it wasn't till about a week later, after I'd been out to the Rez with Harvey a few times, that I met Dave.

I was in the kitchen that afternoon taking a day off from being with Harvey at the Rez when I saw Dave come out his back door so carefully he didn't let it hit the doorjamb behind him. Despite the ninety-degree heat, Dave wore a plaid, long-sleeve shirt and jeans. He loped across his backyard, jumped the

11

low wooden fence and found a dirt path into the scrublands. His blond crew cut hair shined almost white in the sunlight. My own hair was huge on my head—a brown, curly, "Jew-fro." I had stopped shaving when I turned seventeen, so I had a moustache and splotchy beard.

Seeing Dave walking away filled my stomach with the queasy butterflies I got when I thought about meeting a new kid. *Don't be such a wuss*, I thought. *Go talk to this guy.*

I set my Coke bottle down, got my feet to move, and followed Dave out into the scrublands, though by the time I got into all the trees and bushes I had lost him. Birds chirped and wind touched my face and arms as I climbed a short hill and then walked deeper into the locust and mesquite trees.

Following sneaker prints I hoped were Dave's, I walked past junk piles, abandoned cars and bikes, broken bottles and trash. A young kid yelled "beep beep" to warn me off the trail, and I jumped over as he shot past on his yellow and red Stingray bicycle. Far to my left there was a rumbling sound, a semi-truck moving west on the arterial beyond the scrublands, Florida Road.

Standing here at a nexus of dozens of dirt trails—some well-worn by bicycles and others almost nonexistent like deer trails branching off in every direction—I sweated but panted less than a week ago. Following the sneaker prints to the east, I saw them veer north into a thicket of bushes that would cut my arms if I walked through them. Dave had clearly gone this way though, so I picked gingerly through the bushes, getting tiny cuts on my arms then passing through and coming to big piles of debris—old plywood, machine parts, whole rusted cars as the base, everything piled higher than anywhere else in these scrublands.

Where had Dave gone, I wondered. Searching this way and that way, I couldn't spot shoe prints anymore, as if they'd just— poof!—disappeared at the edge of these piles.

Then I heard what sounded like music. Where was it coming from? The other side of the piles? To get there, I would have to climb over, but since I only had on my leather sandals, I could easily hurt myself on the rusted nails that jutted out from wood in the junk piles. My best alternative was to go up and over a twenty-foot boulder, one of three boulders that abutted the piles.

"Do it, Ben," I motivated myself in a kind of whisper. Jumping onto the boulder, I crooked my toes into tiny rock nubs, grabbed a protrusion in the rock with my right fingers, then my left, and kept doing this until my toes and fingers were sore. Finally, I got to the thin fault line at the top and pulled myself up to the top of the boulder. From this perch, I heard the music more clearly, "Jumping Jack Flash" by the Rolling Stones playing from a tinny radio to my right.

I climbed down the other side of the boulder, dropped to the ground and shook dirt out of my sandals. Avoiding a prickly holly bush, I came to another dense stand of trees and bushes and discovered a dome-like fort pushed against a low rock wall. It was shaped like an igloo or even a sweat lodge, like the one I had seen out on the Rez.

Had Dave built this, I wondered?

Covering the whole igloo structure—except for the door which was just a flap of gray army tarpaulin—were old blankets, quilts, tarps, and tree branches. If Dave had built this, he did a good job with what he had around him in the junk piles and forest.

I walked up to the flap-door and dropped down to my knees. Inside the fort I saw Dave McConnell sitting lotus style on cardboard flooring, his tongue tip jutting out the left side of his lips as he wrote in a thick blue spiral notebook.

He saw my shadow immediately and clamped his book shut.

"Sorry, man," I apologized.

"Jesus Christ!" His cheeks flushed so red I could see them change color even with the cave-like darkness.

13

I stepped back, continuing to mutter, "Sorry, sorry."

As he crawled toward the doorway, I saw the blue spiral notebook on the dirt floor, a yellow paperback novel, a flashlight, a plastic bag, pieces of cardboard stacked next to the door, and a silver-and-black transistor radio.

"When did you build this . . . fort?" I asked. "It's cool."

"You scared me, man," he said.

Without answering my question, he stood up, brushed his butt with both hands, and took a position in front of the door like a sentinel. He stood an inch or two shorter than me and wore a white t-shirt under his plaid shirt.

"Sorry, man," I apologized once again. "You're Dave McConnell, though, right?"

He nodded and swallowed hard, his Adam's apple bobbing under the almost translucent white skin of his throat.

"I'm Ben Brickman," I said, putting out my hand. His handshake, clammy, came and went rapidly. "I got here a week ago, from New York."

"You're Harvey Brickman's son," he confirmed.

"Your Mom's originally from Queens, right?" I asked, trying to make conversation, both of us swaying on our feet.

"Yeah. Astoria. Her mom's side is Jewish. I've been to Queens a couple times."

He looked like a one-hundred-pound-weakling kid, but his blue eyes with flecks of gold appeared very adult. As pale as he was, he didn't look Jewish at all and he seemed even more shy and nervous than Harvey had described.

"What grade you in?" I asked.

"I'll be a junior," he said, lifting his right hand to bite at his thumb.

"You sixteen or seventeen?"

He shrugged. "Sixteen. Just turned. You're seventeen?"

I nodded and cocked my head to the fort. "You writing in there? A journal?"

This question made him frown, even look angry. His thin lips closed tight, his hands went back down at his sides. Three lines formed across his forehead as his eyelids closed slightly over his blue eyes.

"Kind of, yeah."

It wasn't anger, though, I decided quickly—this was just how he concentrated.

"I keep a journal, too, sometimes," I nodded. "What're you reading in there?"

"*Light in August* by William Faulkner," he said.

"Seriously? That's college level stuff."

He didn't respond.

I imagined barging past him and checking his fort and journal out, but his stiff posture said, "I am not inviting you into *my* fort."

"What else you read?" I asked. "You like Hemingway?"

"Sure. I read everything."

His voice squeaked loudly and surprisingly. The puberty squeak shut him up with a new frown as his cheeks flushed again.

"Cool," I nodded, pretending not to notice. I had been through change-of-voice already, and it was no fun.

"You read any plays?"

He shook his head.

I showed off a bit. "Beckett, Leroi Jones, Pinter, Albee, lots of plays are minimalist right now, different from novels like Faulkner."

"Your dad's working on a theater out at the Rez," Dave said. "I've never been out there."

"I'm heading out there again tomorrow. You can come if you want. In fact, your fort looks kind of like a sweat lodge."

"Thanks," he said, noncommittal.

"I did a sweat lodge ceremony with my dad and our friend Eagleclaw on Sunday. It was cool."

"I've never done anything like that," he responded, not proud of it or complaining, just standing there.

"You guys smoke pot out here in the sticks?"

"Sure," he said, but he did not look like a guy who would do that.

We both went silent for a few awkward moments as a commercial for Durango Auto Mart came on the radio. This town in the mountains only had 10,000 residents in it, so this Auto Mart was probably one of its biggest car retailers. The commercial wanted people to buy Dodge trucks in a very loud, fake-booming voice.

"Anyway, maybe we'll hang out," I said. "Your house a good place to hang out?"

He shook his head. "My mom's home all the time."

"Harvey's gonna be gone a lot," I shrugged. "I won't be at the Rez every day. You can come over. I've got the basement set up, and Harvey's cool about it."

"Okay," he nodded. "Sure, thanks."

We stood silently for another few awkward seconds, enough time for the commercial to end and The Who's "5:15" to start.

"Anyway, Dave, be cool, okay?" I said. "I'm around."

He seemed to want me to leave, yet I couldn't shake some weird feeling about him, like he also wanted me to stay. My stomach was feeling queasy again, and I decided to respect his turf. I turned and began climbing back up the boulder as Roger Daltrey sang, "Out of my brain on the train."

Back on the other side, I looked up at the top of the boulder and debris piles and thought how weird I was to be scared of some geeky artistic kid. What a wuss I was. I panted loudly a few times while noting two good landmarks to memorize—six branches of a juniper tree pointing upward and a gap of dirt and sand at the trail's edge. With these landmarks in my head, I could come back to this fort sometime, just to check it out more.

I wanted to see what he wrote in that blue spiral notebook.

Dave's face had showed such fear when I caught him.

# CHAPTER 2

"BOUNDARIES, BEN!" my mother lectured me. "You absolutely do not need to know what is in that journal!"

Standing in the gold kitchen—my father sitting at the long dining room table a few feet away—I told her about meeting Dave. She sat, I knew, at our little table off the kitchen in our apartment back on 34th Street between Third Avenue and Lexington.

"Not even a little?" I joked.

"Not even a little," she insisted.

She would be smoking a cigarette, the smoke curling upward, her typewriter on the table, papers all around her.

"Okay," I promised. "I'll leave it alone."

Satisfied, she got back to talking about her classes and a study on depression she and two colleagues were doing with their students. We were a typical single mother and son who loved each other, though it didn't hurt me to have some space. She often told me that it was good for me to "have some father-son time."

Before we hung up, she asked whether Harvey fed me well enough.

"Harvey, do you feed me well enough?" I called out to him.

"Boundaries, Ben!" she admonished. "I asked *you*, not him!"

As Harvey called back, "Tell her I don't feed you at all," I said to my mother, "I was joking, geez." She laughed, and we hung up.

That evening, I did sneak back to Dave's fort, despite my mother's admonition. It was almost nighttime when I watched him go into his house. After I waited a bit to make sure it was safe,

I snuck out to the trails with a flashlight. I found the juniper tree and dove further into the forest. I wore sneakers this time so the rock wall and boulder would be easier to climb.

Surprisingly, I found nothing in the fort—no journal, books, nothing. I searched the junk piles and all around the boulders and found nothing except trash, debris. He hadn't come back to the house with his stuff, so where had he hid it? Inside the fort was just a dirt floor under the igloo-like dome. I looked around the debris piles but still didn't see stuff.

It was weird of me to search through the fort, I thought, but I did it for some reason I couldn't define. Maybe Dave and I weren't meant to be friends, I pondered. Maybe I did have some kind of "problem with boundaries," like my mother said. Or maybe I was just curious why I had weird feelings when this kid looked at me.

The next day, I forgot all that—at least for a while. It was around three in the afternoon, and Harvey hadn't come home yet. I was down in the basement. I had lit candles and a stick of incense every day for the moldy smell that lingered down there. ELP's *Trilogy* played on the record player, the piano and guitar gearing up loudly as I stood on a chair and unhooked the humming overhead fluorescent light. Stepping back down, the job done, I thought I heard the doorbell ring and raced upstairs two steps at a time to check.

Dave stood at the screen door holding a pie in his hands. Bert McConnell stood next to him. Father and son looked alike at the top—both with the blond crew cuts given to them by their barber, Molly McConnell—but Bert, a lawyer, wore a blue polyester suit with blue vest and flair slacks, very different than Dave.

"Did you guys ring the doorbell?" I asked stupidly.

"Three times," Bert responded. He had blue eyes like his son, but there were no gold flecks in them. "I'm Bert McConnell. You can call me Bert. Your father told me kids in New York are calling their parents by their first names now."

His tone needed sloughing off, so I just said, "Yeah. Good to finally meet you, Bert," emphasizing his first name in a twitch of rebellion as I opened the screen door for the two of them. I felt like these two people were pretty stiff with one another, like a father and son at war. Did Bert force Dave to come over here with him? As I stepped back, Bert offered his hand in a very strong handshake, far more so than his son's, and not clammy.

"Molly—Dave's mother—wants you to have this pie as a welcome to the neighborhood, kind of like the welcome wagon," he said, but without humor.

"Thanks," I answered automatically. Dave's mom had covered the pie with a thin white cloth now stained red from the leaking berries. The pan was still hot enough that I had to hold it with the same white potholder underneath its base that Dave had passed to me.

"Harvey should be home pretty soon," I said.

"I'll leave you two to get to know each other," Bert said. He seemed to talk abruptly, shy like his son. His forehead also crinkled in the same frowning lines Dave got when he concentrated, three furrows horizontal across his forehead, eyes half closing.

"Leave some pie for Harvey," he ordered as the screen door slapped shut behind him. I watched him move down the steps, a small-town Western type who probably saw me as a hippie kid. He probably didn't like me but wanted his shy and geeky son to have a friend.

"Our folks sure want us to be friends," I joked with Dave, walking with him to the kitchen.

"I guess," Dave replied, standing against the counter with his hands in his pockets and shoulders slumped. "It's because we both want to be writers. That's what your father told me a couple weeks ago."

"Sounds like Harvey. You want to get stoned and eat pie?" I asked, getting a knife from the drawer.

"Get stoned now?" His face narrowed as if he couldn't believe I would ask him such a dangerous question.

"I got the basement set up right," I shrugged. "Harvey'll be back from the Rez in a while, but he doesn't care what I do."

Licking the knife, I tasted strawberry-rhubarb.

"Come on. I'll show you my Bat Cave."

Walking past, I smelled something on him, maybe cologne? He followed me, and I thought he was aloof, even a bit arrogant, but he also seemed to act like a little kid, a follower, like how he cut his hair to follow after his dad, or how he followed me down the basement steps, both of us clomping on the wood, his sneakers louder than my bare feet.

"Whoa, I could never do this in my folks' house," Dave admitted when we got to the bottom of the stairs. "*Mirabile dictum,* Ben."

"Is that Latin?" I asked, putting the pie on the little table in front of the couch.

"Yeah, I know a little."

"You go to Catholic school?"

"I did," he shrugged, "until middle school. Plus, I had a piano teacher. He was a priest. He taught me."

I moved to the wall to take my baggie of dope out from behind my record albums.

"*Mirabile dictum* basically means, 'that's amazing' or 'that's cool,'" he said.

I still remembered some Hindi from when my folks lived in India, and I knew some Hebrew from my bar mitzvah, but I never found ways to use the stuff in conversation.

"I want to understand William Faulkner's Latinate vocabulary," Dave said as I came back to the couch, "so what I do is, I tape lists of vocabulary words and Latin phrases on my bedroom wall, then I memorize them when I go to bed and try to use them in stories the next day. I want to write like Faulkner, but I mainly write science fiction."

*William Faulkner's Latinate vocabulary?*

"I'm kind of weird, I know," he admitted, sensing my skepticism.

"No, that's cool," I self-corrected, smiling away my judgmental face. "I want to do something big too. Like, I want to try all the world's religions before I'm twenty-five." I pulled out my tiny ceramic pot pipe from the plastic bag. "After that, I'll probably be a writer, but maybe a psychologist, or maybe I'll become the first Jewish president," I chuckled. "But my parents and me, we don't really go to synagogue anymore, so the Jewish part would be suspicious. But you already absolutely know what you want to be, a writer. That's cool."

"But not a Catholic writer," he said. "Not any kind except myself. My mom and dad go to church still, but I don't."

"Huh," I acknowledged, seeing the pattern already, how he wanted to follow me in my abandonment of going to synagogue by showing that he no longer went to his Catholic church.

Lighting the pipe with my blue Bic lighter, I sucked in, then, after a pause, shot smoke out so that a cloud surrounded us. "All I know is, I'm a Fantasarian," I said.

His head cocked slightly to the side, measuring the word. I handed him the tiny pipe and he studied it. I could tell he wasn't sure he wanted to smoke.

"It's a word my friend Jeremy and I invented," I said, giving him time. "It means that we make our own world. The arts and spirituality are the two fields that are gonna be crucial in the new age. We're all about that. Even technology is gonna be about fantasy and making new worlds that are different from this messed up world. And when we're adults, we won't screw things up like things are now with all the crap adults do. That's a Fantasarian."

"I want to write science fiction novels, a whole series," he nodded as the pipe lost its flame. "My big dream is to write a huge Bible, maybe call it the Third Testament, and it takes place inside a computer, like in a Philip K. Dick novel but written by Faulkner. The computer's world will be every single planet, and no adult thought it up. It's a kid who thought up the whole world, the whole Bible, everything, and everything alive is really what one kid is imagining."

He stopped a moment to look at me. "So, I'm a Fantasarian, right?"

"That qualifies," I chuckled.

My stomach had been queasy and nervous with him and his dad, but now that I was warming up to him I realized that my nervousness wasn't just because I was meeting someone new, but because I was embarrassed that I wanted him—this artistic weirdo—to be my friend. I'd been lonely the past week, the kids at the Rez basically staying away from me, a white kid, so I went after this weird guy, and now that we were getting stoned together— one of the things I always did to make a new friend—I felt guilty that I had wanted to pry into his life and see his journal. To cover up my nervousness, I asked him, "You sure you've never smoked dope before? Your computer-bible idea sounds really stoner."

"I don't get stoned," he confessed. "Can you teach me?" His eyes searched mine, something he didn't seem to do much—look someone in the eye. I thought a minute ago he had sounded mature, but now he sounded like a little brother again.

"Okay. Give the pipe here. I never took Latin," I said, taking the pipe out of his hand, "and I couldn't write about the whole Bible or anything, but I grok what you're saying. You know that word, grok, right?"

I turned back to him as I put a piece of bud in the pipe.

"I grok that," he nodded, recognizing the Robert Heinlein word from *Stranger in a Strange Land.*

We raised our hands simultaneously for a high five, grinning at our synchronicity. I used my Bic lighter to light the pipe again, inhaled the smoke, then gave the pipe back to Dave.

"Just suck it in like a cigarette," I taught, while smoke came out of my nose and mouth. "Don't worry if you cough. Coughing makes the dope go into your head, so coughing's okay."

Dave bravely sucked on the pipe, held the dope in his lungs for a second, then his eyes went wide as he coughed it all out.

Grabbing the pipe from Dave's convulsing hands, I laughed, "No problem, happens to everyone."

As Dave continued coughing, I walked over to the record player and replaced ELP's *Trilogy* with Supertramp's *Crime of the Century* , then moved back to the couch. We sang along to the music and Dave tried the dope again, holding more smoke in his lungs for longer than before and coughing less. Then we got the munchies, so we ate the strawberry and rhubarb pie. I noticed that Dave's hand shook a little bit while raising the fork to his mouth.

Dave said he heard that I did accents, so I showed him some of my best ones—my Long Island Jewish accent, my Italian mafia Don Corleone accent, my French accent, my Hindu accent. Then I did my Texas drawl, saying, "Don't squat with yer spurs on, kid."

Dave laughed at my Texas accent more loudly than I thought he could laugh. He wanted me to do more of that one, so I did.

"By the way, man, how come you cut your hair so short?" I asked him after I got tired of doing it. "You had long hair the first time I saw you."

"I did it myself and my mom freaked out," he said without really answering the question. "I cut myself right here." He showed me his right hand where a little cut was healing. "It's the same spot where Tom Sawyer and Huck Finn made their blood pact," he said. My stoned brain thought that was a cool coincidence, since we were just becoming friends.

"I need more dope," he said, reaching for the pipe. "You want more too?"

I got the pipe going, my stomach no longer queasy. Dave took a little toke and then pointed to my copy of Hermann Hesse's *Siddhartha* on the book shelf.

"Maybe you'll be Siddhartha and I'll be Govinda," he said.

"Ha," I laughed like a real stoner.

Suddenly we heard creaking above us. Harvey. Dave got frightened, like we had to hide the dope.

I shook my head. "Don't worry, man. Harvey's cool."

As if on cue, Harvey knocked on the basement door above us.

"It's open," I called up.

Coming downstairs, he opened his arms wide. "Great to see you, Dave! I'm so glad you guys found each other." He saw that we were stoned and didn't ask many questions, just went back upstairs, taking the empty pie pan with him.

When Dave finally had to leave, I got him some Visine and then watched him glide down the sidewalk with his arms waving back and forth like a dork. He must get beat up by older boys a lot, I thought. I wondered if there was any chance that I walked like that.

I turned into the dining room and saw Harvey sitting at the table with his old leather briefcase and scripts and spreadsheets taking up most of the table. He asked me how I liked Dave.

"He's okay," I shrugged. "Nerdy, shy, knows Latin, which is kind of weird, in a hick town like this, don't you think?"

"Durango constantly surprises me," he shrugged. "It's got every kind of person in it—hippies, rednecks, cowboys, Indians. It's not New York, but it's more than you think."

He stood and moved to the kitchen, focusing on the refrigerator. "What should we do tonight?" he asked. "Gourmet dinner?"

That meant TV dinners.

"Sure," I nodded.

As Harvey continued rummaging through the fridge, I felt happy that I'd met someone, like I could be a good big brother to a total nerd like Dave McConnell.

# CHAPTER 3

THE NEXT FRIDAY AFTERNOON, Dave's parents gave him permission to sleep over and he suggested that we take our sleeping bags to an abandoned farm he wanted to show me. When Harvey heard about our idea, he asked if we could deliver a box of props to the Reservation on our way. The Rez was thirty miles past where Dave wanted us to go, but we said sure. I wanted to introduce Dave to Eagleclaw—John Eagleclaw Simpson—anyway and show him the sweat lodge that looked so much like his fort in the scrublands. So we loaded the up the car with boxes and supplies and then headed east out of town toward Ignacio.

Wind hit my face and levitating hand as we drove past ranches with chestnut horses grazing in low-nub summer grass, cows huddling in the small shade of an oak or maple tree. Farther southeast the land turned to desert with cacti that appeared almost human with their spiky arms and heads. I pointed out to Dave the huge sign to welcome visitors. Someone had crossed out "Reservation" with black spray paint and scrawled "Prison" in its place.

"Here we go," I said, turning right toward a crop of houses and two school buildings—the school house and gym. I pointed to silos and buildings a mile farther down the road. "That's Ignacio," I said as we slowed down to five miles an hour, turned right, followed a pickup truck filled with Indian kids.

Dave looked out the windshield at the houses in this area, run-down, paint peeling all over them, roof shakes falling off—only

27

one house and yard kept up well, with an old wagon out front, painted bright green. Some little girls played jump rope in that yard and a mom hung clothes on a clothesline.

"Okay, folks," I announced, imitating what Harvey liked to say to the theater troupe. "Let's get to work."

I pulled the Dart just beside the entrance of the gym. Above its big wide doors, a sign said: "William Red Eagle Pritchard High School. The Coyotes."

We got out of the car and some Indians there saw us, coming to the car. Carrying the boxes, we entered the gym where I introduced Dave to Robert Carlson, Tom Red Feather, Cary Louise, Corkey Anderson. Dave seemed nervous, clammy-handed, biting his thumb. Robert took us outside to help build part of a set where we held boards and hammered where instructed. "Your dad taking a break today?" Robert asked. I said yes and he joked, "We all need a break from this group." There was so much drinking in the troupe, it scared Harvey sometimes. "I'm not sure if we're going to pull this off," he had said sadly to me more than once.

When Robert asked Dave what the "new white boy" thought of the reservation, Dave said, "It's cool," trying to appear nonchalant. "This is my first time out here," he said, then turned red, immediately embarrassed for sounding like a dork.

The Indians laughed but I said, "Dave's a smart kid, watch out," as if that meant something, and the Indian men turned away. We walked into the gym, and Cary Louise asked how my father was doing. She was a tall, beautiful Indian woman, about thirty, and dressed in slacks and a white blouse with the outline of her breasts behind the cloth. I had thought for the last week that she liked Harvey in a romantic way, but he said he hadn't noticed.

Dave sat down on one of the bleachers while Cary Louise yelled at a few older boys and men in their twenties playing basketball at the other end of the gym to quiet down. Closer to us, between the stage and the basketball players, Indian women and one white woman were making alterations to costumes. Two of the women had straight pins in their mouths and all the women worked around a large clothes-draped table. There was a piano to their left, against the bleachers on that side, and I saw Dave look at it.

"Why don't you play something?" I pointed to the piano, coming up to him with a sandwich. I knew he had been really good once. When Molly and Bert invited us over to their house for dinner one night, "to get to know one another," Molly and Dave played a piano duet on their big Steinway.

Dave shrugged, eating his sandwich, then decided it was okay to play. Walking to the piano, he stood a second fighting his own nervousness. When he finally sat down on the piano bench, he started playing music slow and low, like he didn't want anyone to hear. He looked over at me more than once, like he wanted to make sure I was looking, then he played a little louder, then a little louder and a little faster, and pretty soon other people stopped what they were doing to listen.

Even the basketball players stopped. Cary Louise came over to me and touched my shoulder, making my body tingle. "Ben, did you know he could play like that?"

I nodded. "Yeah, kind of."

"It's Brahms' *Piano Concerto Number 2*," she said, "not an easy piece of music."

Dave finished playing and some of the people applauded. Dave took a quick, shy, red-faced bow. I high fived him and he high fived me back and his face stayed red for a while as we got in the car and drove further east toward John Eagleclaw Simpson's house. We talked a bit while I drove, then just became silent looking at the desert. At a rise in the road, we could see Eagleclaw's pond and house.

"There it is," I pointed, and Dave saw what I had seen the first time out here, how this very smart guy, very old, with a Master's Degree in Theater, an elder of the tribe, a playwright, who had lived with us in New York for a couple months while studying at NYU, lived here on a bunch of land that, from the front, looked like squalor—trash everywhere, rusted cars and refrigerators, chickens walking and pecking, no grass just weeds. I knew behind the house, down by the pond and sweat lodge, Eagleclaw kept things cleaner, but not here, not even at his front door, which was faded wood with no doorbell or anything pretty.

Eagleclaw came to the door in his usual "home" clothing—dirty sandals, long black shorts, and open short sleeve shirt showing his brown hairless chest and little paunch of a stomach. He was in his early seventies and wore thick, coke bottle glasses with black frames, his long black and gray hair pulled back in a braided pony-tail. He wobbled when he walked from back problems and bow legs and pain, but he liked to shake hands and had a strong handshake.

"It is good to finally meet you," he said to Dave, his voice always slow, almost formal, but friendly as Dave pulled his hand away. "Ben has spoken of you. He says you have built a sweat lodge in some scrublands." Eagleclaw's voice was deep with an accent, an Indian or Native American or Southern Ute accent I had trouble imitating because it was in no way exaggerated.

"No, it's just a fort," Dave corrected. "I've never seen a sweat lodge before."

"Have you boys eaten?" Eagleclaw asked as we walked into his house. Some of the rooms were finished but some of them were still in the process of being built or remodeled—a kind of permanent, dusty, tools-spread-everywhere project for this nice old man who lived alone and liked to fix things and keep busy.

I said we already ate, suggesting we look at the sweat lodge.

We chatted as we walked down the path towards the pond and the outbuildings, one of them a shelter that housed wood and another covering a round dome that looked very much like Dave's fort.

Sitting down on folding chairs we drank some iced tea Eagleclaw had handed me to carry down, using dirty cups he kept next to the lodge. He talked about how it was "meant to be" that one day Dave should sweat with us, especially because "the ancestors and the spirits have already invited Dave McConnell into the lodge, obviously." Dave agreed to sweat "some day."

* * *

"He's cool," Dave said as we drove away from the Rez, back toward the place Dave wanted to show me, where we would spend the night.

"Is it weird or what, your fort and that lodge?" I asked. "They look so similar. It must be meant to be."

"I guess," Dave shrugged. "But I'm not gonna do a sweat right away. I'd be too nervous. I have to build up to it."

"You sure you never went to the Rez?" I asked him again.

No, he shrugged. "You guys really go naked in that place?" he asked.

Dave had focused on this specifically more than once in the last week. Earlier today, when Eagleclaw described a sweat lodge ceremony, Dave's first question was whether all the guys would have to be naked. Eagleclaw assured him they didn't have to be. "Some men in our men's sweats prefer to be naked with mother earth, but most are more modest." Going naked didn't bother me or Harvey, I told Dave, because we were theater people—exhibitionists.

"No way!" He had seemed shocked the first time he heard I went naked with all those older guys. I didn't tell Dave it made me

31

queasy and I didn't try to explain that going in there naked was a challenge for me—I wanted to not be afraid of anything, thinking that if I could be fearless I would meet God or the ancestors or the spirits.

"Check out that cactus," Dave pointed.

"Which?" There were lots of them as we passed.

"Pull over."

Dave had an idea, so I pulled over. "What's up?"

"You'll see."

We got out of the car, and I followed Dave through some dirt to a huge cactus about ten feet tall with three long arms. On one of the arms, he reached out and ran the tip of his index finger against a thorn so that it drew blood. "Let's be blood brothers," he said, showing me the leak of blood on his finger.

I grinned and pricked my finger. Then we rubbed our fingers together until our blood was mixed and impossible to tell apart. "We're officially blood brothers," he said.

"Like Tom Sawyer and Huckleberry Finn," I said.

"Yeah!" he grinned, holding his hand up for a high five.

We laughed and got back in the car, listening to the radio as we drove past farms and ranches for about twenty-five miles. Then he had me make some turns and we came to our destination, an abandoned farm once owned by the Lester family, Dave said. They had been good friends of the McConnells, with kids the same age and all that, but they lost the farm to bankruptcy and had to move to Michigan where they had relatives.

This abandoned place was cool, a hundred acres of scraggly fields with a ruined house on the south side surrounded by trees. Near the house was a big barn with a collapsing roof and empty horse stalls in the back. That's where Dave told me to park. We unloaded what little we had, some sandwiches, two sleeping bags, some water, and started a fire. As it got dark, we sat on small mounds of sawdust next to the fire passing a pipe back and forth and eating peanut butter sandwiches, a whole bag of Ruffles potato chips, and another bag of M & Ms. Then we lay back in the moonlight that flowed down through the massive holes in the barn roof.

"Ben, I think you are Captain Kirk and I'm Mr. Spock," Dave announced, stoned.

"Okay," I quipped. "But I thought we were Huck Finn and Tom Sawyer."

"We are." He nodded his head, very focused, the firelight making his cheeks look red. "I've decided to save money for college in New York. I want to go to NYU like you. We could be roommates, and you could show me around New York. We could be like Reuven and Danny Saunders in *The Chosen*. What do you think? I wouldn't be any trouble."

I looked over at him, joking again, "Now we're Reuven and Danny?" but then I caught up to his last part. "Wait, what do you mean? You can be trouble if you want."

"Okay," he grinned. "I'll be trouble." I didn't know what that meant exactly. I could just barely see his blue eyes with their little gold flecks in the moonlight.

"And wait again," I said, "Which one am I—Reuven or Danny?"

"I don't know. Good question."

"You're the brilliant math piano Latin genius, so you're probably Danny."

He shrugged again. "But you can do accents and you're a great actor, so maybe you're Danny. Anyway, blood brother, I'll be whichever one you want. You pick."

I laughed, rolling over on top of him to wrestle.

"You're really coming out of your shell, man. You're like a kid but you're also way older than your age. You're unique, bro. That's for sure."

"I've never had a friend like you," he said, not trying to push me off. "We could do anything together. We're like . . . we could have been in the same platoon in Vietnam, maybe. We'd fight everyone. Did I ever tell you about Red McConnell, my cousin?"

I hadn't heard about him before. I rolled off Dave so he could tell me.

"Red was my dad's favorite cousin. He wishes Red was his son, not me," Dave reported in an analytical mode. "I liked Red too, but he came back from Vietnam and shot himself."

"Jesus!" I said, caught by surprise.

Dave apologized for springing it on me.

"He really did that?" I asked.

Dave shrugged silently, affirmatively, traveling elsewhere for a moment, over to wherever he thought his cousin had gone. Then he said he was tired and looked at his watch. It was almost midnight already. I lit the pipe for a last toke as Dave pulled off his plaid shirt and then his white undershirt. He seemed to want to put his pajama top on real fast but then stopped to let his chest and arms stay naked.

"I think I just need to show you something," he said. "I hope you decide to stay my friend." He lifted his long arms into the air like he was being arrested and showed me his pale, skinny torso. In the moonlight, I could see that he had no hair under his skinny arms, or anywhere on his emaciated chest.

"I'm sixteen, but I've got no hair," he confessed, moving the point of his chin back and forth to each arm pit. "That's why I wear lots of clothes. It's not just my zits. It's because I'm sixteen, but I'm pretty far away from being a man."

I cocked my head downward. "You've got no hair, even on the privates?"

He shook his head. "That's why I'm embarrassed to go up to

the lake with you or go naked in the sweat lodge at the reservation. I'm still like a little boy."

"Nah, man. It's okay."

Pulling his pajama top on, he asked, "Will you still be my friend? Will you still let me hang out with you?"

This fear must be why he made all the comparisons to best friends, like Huck Finn or Govinda or Mr. Spock, I thought.

"Of course, man. Some boys don't get hair yet, but they're still brilliant. Don't take stuff so seriously."

My last comment seemed to make him reflect on something bad as I searched for more words to reassure him.

"You're just a late bloomer," I shrugged. "It's in your genes or something. There's lot of kinds of guys in the world, with different bodies."

"Not like me," he frowned. "I'm the only sixteen-year-old in gym class with no hair. I want hair like you have."

He paused a beat and then pointed to me sitting on top of my sleeping bag dressed just in my blue and white boxers.

"Can I touch your hair, Ben? On your chest. Nowhere else," he reassured me.

Before I could say no to this strange request, I said, "Okay, I guess."

Quickly, before I changed my mind, he reached his right palm towards my chest. My stomach got queasy as his cold palm pressed gently into the hairy dent between my nipples. He seemed to shiver when he pulled away, and my stomach turned over.

"Maybe I'll never get hair," he said sadly, though with some other tone mixed in that I couldn't figure out. "It's why I cut my hair so short, you know. Because maybe I shouldn't ever get hair."

"Bro, you're scared of too much, and you think weird stuff," I said. "You know what you should do? You should do whatever you're the most scared of. Even if kids mess with you, you should

35

just be yourself, you know? I mean, you can't let other people control your thoughts. You have to be a free spirit."

I was starting to sound cheesy, but he nodded anyway.

"Maybe," he said.

"Anyway, don't worry so much!" I laughed, getting into my sleeping bag. "When we're old men, we'll be like Harvey and Bert, with hair growing out our ears. Believe me, we'll wish we had *less* hair."

I could still feel the sensation of his hand on my chest as we sang, "I hope I die before I get old," imitating Roger Daltrey of The Who. Dave's voice squeaked which made both of us laugh. Then we were quiet and just looked up at the stars and the moon. A few minutes later, Dave started snoring. I was just about asleep when I heard Dave moan and mumble, "No, no."

I turned my body and leaned on my elbows to face him.

"Stop," he hissed. He mumbled some more words I couldn't understand and then suddenly flinched his body and cried, "Allen, stop!"

"Dave," I whispered.

His body jerked more, like he was convulsing.

He was clearly dreaming some really bad stuff.

"Allen, I'm sorry!" he called out.

He looked like he was sweating, and I touched his forehead, searching for a fever like my mom had done many times with me.

"No, no!" he jerked his body.

I was getting worried. I pushed at Dave's shoulder to wake him.

"No!" he yelled. He continued shuddering, so I climbed out of my sleeping bag and grabbed him more forcefully. "Dave, it's okay. It's just a bad dream, man."

Finally, he stopped moving, though he didn't wake up.

I stared at him in the dark for a while, then slid back into my sleeping bag.

Who was this Allen guy?

He must have done something very bad to Dave.

# CHAPTER 4

THE NEXT DAY as I was doing my chores at home—mowing the lawn, sweeping the porch, washing the dishes—I rehearsed how I might ask Dave about who Allen was and what he'd done to him. My stomach kept getting queasier as I rehearsed. What if Dave harbored a big secret about this Allen guy? What if Dave got mad that I knew the secret and our friendship ended?

The afternoon got very hot, and I felt almost crazy when Dave finally came over around two o'clock. I was in the kitchen getting some orange juice.

"Hey, Dave," I said, trying to act nonchalant. "You want some OJ?"

"Sure," he said.

As we drank, he told me how emotional his dad had been during their practice driving session that afternoon. He gave me a blow by blow account of driving past the Hanley's barn, one of the places he had shown me, like the Lester's, abandoned since the oil embargo and the recession—and even about going by the graveyard where his grandparents were buried, his father talking about time passing and all that.

But Dave didn't mention last night.

"Bert got emotional about you growing up or something?" I prompted him when he drifted into his usual silence.

"Nah," he shrugged, taking a sip. "His eyes got watery from talking about how he taught Red McConnell how to drive. I really think he loved Red more than me."

"No way," I said reflexively, my mind on Allen and the barn.

"He's proud of you, man. He's got to love you. You're brilliant. You're gonna be famous one day."

Dave stood just a couple feet from me as I replaced the glass pitcher of juice in the fridge. He sniffed the air a couple times and said, "Ben, your breath stinks."

Laughing at his surprising assertiveness, I cupped my hand at my mouth and blew breath into it. I couldn't smell my own bad breath but grinning back at him, I said, "I'll go brush them" and walked up the stairs to the bathroom.

Dave followed me in and, continuing to surprise me, said "I gotta pee," and slid behind me to get to the toilet. I grabbed my toothbrush as Dave unbuckled his belt, lowered his pants and jockey shorts, and peed.

"Whoa man," I joked. "You've finally become brave!"

I slapped his shoulder and he jerked his body and sprayed his pee. We both busted up laughing.

"I trust you completely, man," he told me.

Afterwards, we went down to the basement and played some chess and foosball. Then I played a record and we sat down next to each other on the couch. I kept wanting to ask him about last night and Allen.

Finally, I exhaled. "Dave, I gotta ask you something, okay? You sitting down?"

We grinned at the lame joke while I squirmed around and then just came out with it.

"Look, man. You yelled out in your sleep last night about a guy named Allen."

He seemed shocked. "I talked about Allen in my sleep?"

"You were, like, messed up about him, moaning, flinching. I touched your forehead and it felt like you had a fever."

Raising his hand, he touched his forehead unconsciously. "Really?"

"Who is this guy? Why were you scared of him?"

Dave frowned. "You're my best friend, so I guess I can tell you. He's a bully. He . . . he messed me up a few times."

"What'd he do?"

Dave looked up as Harvey's footsteps passed right above us.

I was worried that Dave wouldn't continue, but he said, "He did . . . all sorts of stuff."

I waited for Dave to go on, and when he hesitated, I asked, "Like what?"

"Bad stuff," Dave replied, bringing his hands back down to his lap and clasping them together. "Allen's a bully with other kids too, but with me he's real mad because his family lost a lot of money because of my dad. He saw me last week and told me he'd mess with me again. I said, 'Not if I mess with you first,' and then I got away from him."

I pulled my legs up under my thighs, lotus style, and turned my body completely to Dave. "He messed with you bad?"

"You're my friend, right?" Dave looked at me directly but also seemed to be looking far away. I thought maybe his chin was quivering a little.

"Of course, man. You can tell me what's going on. I'll help you."

His eyes moved away from mine, towards the foosball table.

"See, the Tremmels make furniture and sell it at their store. People know them pretty well around here. But one time a little girl got hurt when one of their chairs broke. She fell backward off a balcony and broke her back. There was a court case. Bert was the attorney for the plaintiff, the girl's family. Tremmels' insurance had to pay her a hundred thousand dollars. My dad made forty thousand."

"Whoa!"

"Mom says we paid off our house from it. That's when we got the new pickup. Anyway, Allen pantsed me a couple times after that and then one time . . ."

Dave went silent for a second, then breathed in and looked me in the eyes again.

"I feel weird telling you all this. It's gross."

Leaning towards him, I said, "You have to tell someone. That's the psychology of bad stuff. You have to talk about it. It's the mature thing to do."

I realized I sounded like a parent, but he didn't seem to mind. His brow creased into three lines and his teeth tugged at his upper lip.

"It's really gross," he said. "You ever been messed with by guys, when you were younger?"

"Of course," I said honestly. "Every boy has, sometime or another. But was it pretty bad with Tremmel?"

Dave dropped his eyes, looking at his folded hands on his lap.

"What Allen did to me isn't normal, I don't think. He got some guys to hold me down in the locker room and he took a razor to my . . . you know . . . my . . . privates. I was really scared, like they were going to cut my nuts off with the razor blade. They made fun of me because I have no hair."

"Whoa."

"But the worst time was at Vallecito Lake. I didn't want to tell you about it."

"It's cool," I encouraged. "I won't tell anyone."

He paused for a few more seconds, getting up courage with each breath, then described how Allen and his friends had grabbed him by the hair and held him down and tried to push his fishing pole into his butthole, though never penetrating he assured me, because the boys were interrupted. As he described everything, Dave kept looking at his hands and feet. His tone was droning as he tried not to cry.

"Jesus, man," I muttered as I bounced with tension. "Another split second and Allen would've cornholed you with the pole? No wonder you hate that lake." Harvey and I had gone up there to swim once, and I had hitchhiked up there once myself. Both times Dave had said he didn't want to go.

"Yeah," he murmured, head down.

I jumped off the couch and moved to the closet and kicked karate kicks at the door.

"That prick, Tremmel!" I shouted, not just to be sympathetic but because something was happening inside me. Memories began to flood like a huge hand sweeping across the sky, horizon to horizon, erasing everything, replacing everything. I moved to the foosball table with my Ben Brickman mask tight on my face, but inside I was naked in New York, on Lexington Avenue, in a doctor's office.

Dave was watching me, trying to read my body language.

"You can't tell anyone," he said. "No one. You know that, right?"

"Of course! You know why I like you, man? Because you have courage, you're honest, you don't hide bad stuff inside you, you talk about it. Bullies are just insecure assholes who mess with smart guys because they're insecure."

I was moving around the room, pacing, lecturing.

"That's the psychology of it, that's their problem, but you've got talent, man, you're smart."

I pointed at Dave.

"Telling the truth is cool. Not everyone can do it."

"Thanks, man."

"I bet it was Allen and his assholes who put you in your shell, Dave, but you can't let the world take the magic out of you."

The words again sounded lame and cliché, but Dave smiled anyway. "Yeah. The magic. Thanks, man."

He joined me at the foosball table, and we each grabbed two toggles.

"Man, I'm glad you told me this," I said, breathing hard, almost panting.

Dave dropped the ball down into the middle of the foosball table, and we played loudly and brutally, my brain like a blob I had to keep from exploding by focusing on the little scuffed white ball.

"You know what would be really brave?" he said as he slammed the ball with the legs of a player.

"What, man?" I called, spinning a toggle.

"If we did something to Allen."

"Huh?"

"Yeah, like, maybe do something to him that would stop him from doing bad stuff to other kids. It could be like a sacred mission."

"A sacred mission?" I repeated, my mind elsewhere.

"Yeah, like what if I could hurt him so bad he'll think twice about ever hurting anyone again, including me? That would be noble, right? Like in *Kung Fu*. He said he was coming after me again, so I have to do something to stop him, right? I just don't know what to do."

"You really think he'll try to mess with you again?" I asked.

Dave stopped playing and shrugged.

"He hates me and he's going to get me again. I know that. I tried talking to him a couple times, but it does no good. Maybe Allen would listen to you? You're strong like he is, and you're a senior."

I moved to the wall, put on a new record, my hand trembling, and then sat down on the couch. Dave followed me, waiting me out. "I don't know, Dave," I said finally. "I don't even know the guy." I hated the weird tone, like pleading or disloyalty, in my voice.

"Allen's a little bigger than you, but you know karate," Dave reasoned. "I want to get him to stop hurting people and I want him to stop pulverizing me and doing stuff to me in the locker room or at the lake. I mean, you know—I don't want to be cornholed or anything."

"Jesus, Dave!"

"Sorry, but you said it earlier, didn't you?"

"Yeah, I know, Dave. Jesus, this is bad."

I agreed with Dave that talking to Allen was probably worthless. Adults love to think that talking to a bully works, but usually it doesn't work at all. Some bullies really need to be fought, like Hitler needed to be fought.

"He touched my privates," Dave continued, "but I'm not a fag. No way. I only get hard-ons from Playboy."

"Dave, I got it. Don't worry about that."

But to show me he was fine, he reached behind my record collection, grabbed one of my hidden Playboys, and opened it to the centerfold.

"You getting a hard-on?" I asked.

"Absolutely," he promised.

"Okay, then," I said, taking the magazine from him. "You're into girls. Don't worry about it."

"You know," Dave said. "Maybe you and I could really do something to Allen—together. Like two Musketeers, with disguises maybe."

I sat next to him and started filling up my pipe, my stomach turning over. "Two Musketeers?"

"Think about it, Ben," he continued. "If someone like you helped me by just holding a gun on Allen, I could beat his naked body with a stick maybe and warn him never to hurt anyone again. Then I'd feel better, and he might not hurt other people anymore. Two birds with one stone. It's weird, I know, but I think about it sometimes.

"Of course, I would never do anything like he did to my . . .

you know . . . privates, except maybe I could hit him in the nuts just once, like he did to me. That might be okay. Then we could tell him we'd always find him if he did anymore bad bullying things, then we'd run away. We'd be in disguise, so he wouldn't know it's us. We could look like men, especially if I didn't talk and—"

I interrupted him. "Dave, it's normal to want revenge, but guns, man? That's intense. And beating a naked kid in the nuts? That's not good, man."

I watched smoke curl upward.

"My father has a gun, so does Eagleclaw. All the men have guns around here."

"Not my dad," I reminded him.

"Yeah, but . . . Harvey uses them in plays, right? On stage. We could do something like that with Allen. Disguise ourselves like we're in a play. That's what soldiers would do, you know."

He waited a split second, then realized he was being relentless and pulled back a bit.

"Anyway, I don't know . . . it's just a thought."

I took another toke, passed Dave the pipe, and watched him take one.

"I just wish there was a way to be like Carlos Castaneda and get help from the other world to make things balanced in a spiritual way," he said. "I've wanted to fight back for years. I just didn't know anyone who could help me, someone mature like you." He was back in relentless mode.

"I think we should just tell the police about him," I said, trying to be logical, "and maybe tell your dad too since this has to do with that legal case. Maybe he could sue the Tremmels again."

"Are you crazy?" he squeaked, turning a flash of red in the cheeks. "Allen would just deny everything to the police and to my dad! Then he'd kill me or do worse stuff to me."

I saw my stupidity right away but kept trying.

"But maybe the police could find the kids in the locker room and interview them . . ."

I didn't even finish. If the police interviewed everyone in the locker room, or interviewed Stu and Carlos, Dave would just be known as a snitch and a tattletale. He'd get beaten up all the time. I had just said something my mother would say, someone who didn't know anything about what it was like to grow up as a boy.

"The police would be the worst thing," he frowned, "and my father would just call me a wimp."

"Yeah, yeah," I agreed.

He could tell I saw it.

"See, Ben, you got me thinking about the psychology of it when you told me about the naked guys in the sweat lodge. Like, maybe I beat him up while he's naked, and even if his conscious mind doesn't make the connection to the locker room and the lake, his unconscious mind will. That could be the psychology of it."

I shook my head at Dave because I couldn't quite follow this logic but I felt myself also smiling as Dave tried to convince me by using my own words and being so obvious about it.

"Dave," I said, trying another logical track, "you're right about the cops, but I don't think Siddhartha or Quai Chang Kane would hold a gun on a guy and beat him in the nuts. I mean, take Hitler and the Nazis, sure. I wanna kill them all, but you gotta fight a real war in that case. You can't do weird naked stuff to a bully, which just makes you become the bully. That's not what a sweat lodge is about."

Glad I'd spoken like a good big brother, I was confused by what I'd just said. I would have beaten and assassinated Hitler and every Nazi if I'd been in World War II or if they showed up in Durango. The Nazis had killed all my European relatives except one family that escaped to Palestine, so why was I talking to Dave like a coward, telling him he shouldn't do something to such a sicko bully like Tremmel?

"I don't know, Ben," Dave debated, sensing weakness in me. "Moses and God hurt bad people, and Paul said in Corinthians, *In the name of what is true and righteous, God bids you to wield the sword.*"

He put the pot pipe down and turned to me on the couch.

"I think I gotta get Allen out of my head, you know? I don't want to do pervert things to him like shave his privates or anything like that, but I want to do something to him that helps me get his bad stuff out of my head. You get it, don't you, Ben?"

"Yeah, it's called closure," I said. "I do get it." My mind kept wandering into what we were saying and out of it, back to snow falling outside an office window and a boy naked on the couch and a naked hairy man—

"I want to become a great writer," he went on. "But all I can think about is getting Allen out of my head. I should have told you before, since you're my best friend, but I just couldn't. You get that, right?"

"I get it," I murmured, taking another toke.

"And what if Allen did to you what he did to me? Wouldn't you do something back to him, something important, so you could make things right in the world, and in your head? I know I'm the *shy boy*, a pansy weakling and all that, but this basement is part of what I keep thinking about, see. The answer is right here."

He opened his hands wide to take in Harvey's boxes and props.

"Look at this stuff, these props, the costumes. You could direct me in a play or something. Maybe it's not your fight, I get that, but maybe you could help me learn karate enough to use it on Allen. You could help me write a script. I want to be brave. I want to be like you."

"Me?" I scoffed. "I'm not brave."

"Sure, you are," he insisted.

There was so much I could have told him in that instant, but I caught myself.

"Look," I said instead, "You're a good friend, but you can't use these costumes and props. They'd get associated with Harvey. You're not thinking straight, man."

"That's true," he nodded, as if he expected that. "But Allen doesn't know you or your dad. So, it's something to consider. And think about this—my dad did stuff to enemies in Korea, right? So, what if Bert McConnell read a headline in the paper, *Dave McConnell beats up Allen Tremmel?* He might say, 'You're not just a spacey teenager. I'm proud of you.' I mean, Bert wouldn't really read it in the paper, but you know what I mean."

I was seeing things in my head again and I had to move.

"I gotta go pee," I lied. "Hold that thought, man."

Before he could say anything, I climbed the stairs two at a time, went into the hallway bathroom and sat on the toilet, my mind filling up with memories of Dr. Francis and all the disgusting things he forced me to do with him in his office. Tears rose from my stomach into my head and pushed out of my eyes.

"Oh no!"

I covered my mouth to muffle a sudden sob so Harvey wouldn't hear me, Harvey who knew nothing about what happened in that office seven years ago. No one in the whole world knew except Dr. Francis, who took pictures of me and told me it was my turn as I sat naked on the leather couch, my butt cold . . .

"I better get going," I heard Dave say to my father through the door.

"Okay, Dave," he replied. "Say hi to your folks for me."

"Sure," Dave said in his polite way, his sneakers squeaking across the floor and our screen door closing gently behind him.

Not only were so many confusing thoughts and memories swirling inside me, but I realized that I had abandoned Dave after he'd been honest and confided in me about Allen. Maybe he was afraid I was totally weirded out by his confession and was going to tell my father everything he'd said.

No, he trusted me. He knew I wouldn't talk. He was just giving me space.

I hoped so anyways.

When I finally composed myself, I walked out of the bathroom, avoided Harvey, and went quietly back down into the basement.

There was a note from Dave right beside the baggie of dope.

*Sorry I just got so intense. Please don't tell anyone about Allen. You are my best friend. Dave.*

"See, I was right," I said aloud. "He's cool."

Clearly, the kid needed me. And maybe I needed him too. He had just confessed something grosser than gross, so maybe I could finally tell someone about Dr. Francis.

I thought about it a bit more and shook my head. No way. I could not tell him or anybody. Dave had been bullied, but his situation was nothing like my months in the doctor's office. Maybe Dave would think that *I* was the freak for letting Dr. Francis do so many things to me. Maybe Dave wouldn't want to be *my* friend anymore. No way. I couldn't tell him.

And yet a part of me still wanted to.

I put my face into a pillow on the couch and screamed into it till my throat felt like it was torn open.

# CHAPTER 5

IT WAS MY MOTHER who showed me what to do, though she wouldn't have realized it.

I woke up around eleven the next morning and went up to the kitchen and made myself a bowl of Cheerios. While I scarfed it down, my mother called.

"Hi Ben," she said with her croaky cigarette smoking voice. I pictured her blowing smoke out our fifth-story window and looking down at 34th Street in Manhattan. She'd be wearing tight jeans and a sweater even though it was summer.

I made some cheesy joke about our gold phone, and my mom laughed and then asked how Dave was doing.

"He's blossoming," I said, knowing she loved that word.

"That's good to hear. But are you sure he's okay? Harvey worries that he's . . . well . . . perhaps depressed."

"He's fine," I exclaimed, maybe trying to convince myself as much as her. "Why does everyone have to obsess? He's a teenager who's got zits all over him and probably got roughed up by an older kid, but he'll survive. I mean Dave is so friggin' smart, you should hear how he does math equations, or how he can play the piano. He's really incredible. Don't worry. Anyway, how are your *real* patients?"

She skirted that and stayed on Dave. "Ben, it sounds like your protective instincts are coming out with Dave, so if he needs help, help him get it, okay? You are an empathic person. You always have been. You'd make a good psychologist one day, you know."

"Yeah." How many times had she told me this? It seemed like all adults did was repeat themselves.

"I mean, Ben, you've let him through your defenses pretty fast, which is really great. He needs a big brother like you, right? If he is depressed, get him talking about what's going on, okay? You boys just don't talk enough about what you're feeling."

"Jesus, Mom. Everything's okay! Let's talk about something else."

She sensed she needed to back off and went on to tell me all about the Carl Jung article she was working on. I was only half-listening until she wrapped up the call by saying, "I can't tell you how much I miss you. You're the best man I know, Ben."

"Thanks, Mom. I'll be back home soon. I miss you too."

"Okay, I love you."

"I love you too."

I put the gold phone back in the receiver and pressed my stomach inward with both my hands.

How could I love someone as much as I loved her, but also be so angry at her sometimes?

But wasn't she right about some things?

*   *   *

All that next week I felt distracted and worthless. Both Harvey and Dave asked me if something was bugging me, Dave joking that *I* was actually the depressed kid. I assured Harvey that nothing was wrong and told Dave I was "wrestling inside my soul," which meant, he thought, whether or not to help him with Allen. In truth, I was wrestling with the memories in my head of my mother taking me to see the psychiatrist, Dr. Francis.

One night, to help work up my courage, I rode my bike downtown to spy on Allen at his family's furniture store. I saw him in the back, loading couches and other furniture into the backs of people's trucks, helping his dad. He wore blue jeans and cowboy boots and a Tremmel Furniture t-shirt. He and I were about the same size, though he was more muscular. His crew cut hair was blond, and his jaw was long like a blade. My heart started pounding as I noted his resemblance to Dr. Francis. As I rode my bike away from the store, I couldn't help but think that helping Dave get his revenge was meant to be.

I thought about it all week and finally made a decision. I would try to tell Dave some things. I would help him.

The next Saturday night, Dave and I sat on the hood of Harvey's Dodge Dart in the McDonald's parking lot on Main Street. We munched our way through a bag of burgers and fries and watched cars dragging down the road.

"I'm gonna really miss you this fall," I told Dave. "I feel like our souls are like twins. Like we're one soul in two bodies. You know what I mean?"

"Yeah, I feel the same way. I'm definitely coming to New York next year."

"Yeah, man!" I said, revving myself up. "We're blood brothers!"

I held my right hand up for yet another inspirational high five.

Dave slapped my hand and grinned. "Blood brothers!" he agreed.

I slid off the car hood and said, "Listen, blood-brother Dave. I gotta talk to you about something. I finally gotta do it, you know? It's like, related to Allen and you in a way. You opened up to me. Now I gotta open up to you."

He nodded and waited patiently, looking unsurprised. I tried to talk but froze.

Dave prompted me. "You ready to tell me you're gonna help me teach Allen a lesson? Is that it?"

"Yeah, man," I sighed. "You know, I guess so, but this is something else. I feel bad that I haven't told you."

"Told me what?" Dave asked in almost a whisper.

"It's freaky, man. I mean, some stuff happened to me when I was a kid. It might be worse than what Allen did to you."

"Seriously? Like what?"

I looked out onto the street where a Corvette was thundering past and then said, "The point is, you were honest with me, and I've never had a friend like you, not even Jeremy. You're . . . you understand me. There's something about you, man."

The last bit of sunlight illuminated his pale face and zits and blue eyes as he continued to wait patiently for me.

"I gotta be completely vulnerable, like psychology says," I went on. "But maybe without the 'outcome' my mom would want, you know? I mean, moms don't know even half of what's going on."

"That's the truth," he agreed. "What's this about, Ben?"

I tried to tell him but clammed up again.

*Was I a coward? Or was I smart not to say anything, ever?*

I squashed our wrappers and bags into a ball, threw them into a garbage can and opened the car door.

"Come on, Dave. Let's go."

I started the car and sped out toward Highway 3. On the radio the Rolling Stones' "Angie" ended and a deep-voiced jockey promised to play "Goodbye Yellow Brick Road" after a commercial for Montgomery Ward. I didn't want to hear the same loud commercial for the umpteenth time this summer, so I turned down the volume and twisted the Dart off the two-lane highway onto a dirt road. The wheels rumbled over a metal cattle guard as we entered a huge empty field. A quarter mile away, the property owner's house was lit up on a hill, its outline shining under the bright moonlight.

Turning the ignition and headlights off, I looked out of the corner of my eye at Dave who still patiently waited for me to talk, just glancing at me, raising his eyebrows as if to say, "What's up?"

Stepping out of the car, I hissed, "DO IT!"

Dave's body pulsed backward slightly from the shock of my aggressive voice.

"This is gonna change everything," I said. "It's weird, man. It's weirder than your stuff with Allen. Be ready. It's real life, man."

I climbed back up on the hood and then lay down, cupping my hands under my skull. Dave did the same, and we looked up at the silvery moon and the million stars as cicadas sang all around us.

"When I first met you, I thought you were this freaky, zitty, crew-cut kid and that we were, like, totally misfit to be friends," I started. "But there was a reason. God and the spirits and the ancestors brought us together, man."

"You can tell me," Dave said. "I told you my worst thing ever."

"I swear, if you tell anybody anything about what I'm going to tell you, I'll die or I'll have to kill you." I tried to pause in a joking way, but the joke fell lamely in the night and so I got back on track. "No one except you can ever find out. Right?"

"I get it," Dave assured me as I turned to him to get his promise. "I keep secrets. You know that."

"I know, I'm just tripping out." I turned away again, looking up at the sky. "But I gotta tell *somebody*, and you are that somebody, but I'm . . . I'm scared, man."

My stomach had knotted up and I felt close to puking.

"I never told anybody about Allen except you," he reminded me.

I nodded, blew breath out like in a kata I learned from martial arts, then inhaled deeply the smell of grass.

"You know why we can't tell other people about these things?" I said to the night. "Because people who haven't been there, they can't understand. People say they grok what's going on, but they don't, adults especially. Moms, dads—they're in their own universe. If we told them this stuff about how boys really are, they'd think we were gay but we're not, even though we're above all the macho crap and being gay isn't a sin like the religions say, we know that, half the people in theater are gay, but that's not the point, right? That's what's confusing. But the thing is . . ."

My voice was cracking from emotion as I rambled. Looking up at the stars I remembered my mother holding my hand as she walked me to the door that read, *Office of William Francis, M.D.* "He's going to help you, Ben." She had so much hope, and so did I—a kid who hated his parents for getting a divorce and hated himself for causing the divorce.

"So, what happened, man?" Dave encouraged. "Was it a bully?"

I closed my eyes, paused, and finally started.

"What happened was my mom kicked my dad out, and he moved to Vancouver. I was ten. I couldn't handle the whole thing. I got into fights, got suspended from school. I became weird, like there was some other boy inside me. 'An incorrigible and violent boy,' Judith called me. She said I was acting like an animal, not the human being she was raising, ashamed of me. 'You WILL go see a psychiatrist,' she told me. 'You WILL!' So, she took me to see somebody she knew from NYU, Dr. William Francis, who had an office on Lexington Avenue. He was like forty or forty-five, our folks' age. He knew a lot about kids and their 'issues,' Judith said. So anyway, I guess I'm really gonna tell you. Wow. I'm gonna tell you."

"What happened?"

"Well, the first day Dr. Francis seemed cool. He had lots of toys and comic books in his office. He explained the psychology of my outbursts like, 'Benny, you have become anxious and sad because of family instability caused by your parents' divorce. This is why you are acting out in inappropriate ways.'"

"Acting out?" Dave prodded.

"Yeah. Judith had a shadow box in her room with things she collected from all over the world—like little glass animals and stuff, you know?"

"Yeah, okay."

"Well, little Benny Brickman took a baseball bat and pulverized all the little dolphins and birds and tea cups, the whole shadow box. That was the final straw, it tripped my mother out, that's what started me going to Dr. Francis. It kind of tripped me out too. I mean, I was the son of peace-marching, Gandhi-loving parents, right? 'War no more!' 'We shall overcome.' We had the best times at rallies in Central Park—me, my dad, my mom, our friends, even Eagleclaw for a while one year. My parents were totally into it. I loved being in my family back then. But after the divorce, all I wanted to do was beat things to bits. I didn't like it, man, but it was like there was some other animal inside me. You grok that, right?"

"Yeah, of course."

"Anyway, when my mom saw her shadow box with all her heirlooms busted up, it was like she went completely blank, like her love for me was gone. She sent me out of her bedroom and locked the door and cried, and I pounded on the door, trying to get in and tell her I was sorry, but she wouldn't answer. I thought I was so cool, you know, ten years old and breaking everything, but when she was crying and wouldn't talk to me, I knew there was something wrong with me. I had become the bad man, like Harvey was. The psychology of it is weird. It's like the animal became the devil in me, which is just over-talking psychological religious BS, right, but you know what I mean."

"Yeah," Dave nodded.

"So, when Judith said I had to go to a doctor, I didn't argue—and that's crucial information, man." I turned towards him and back away quickly. "See, I didn't put up a fight. I just went to Dr. Francis and kind of liked him at first. He had a nice office that smelled like cologne and we sat on the couch and he explained how my unconscious mind was overwhelming my conscious mind and how I didn't get the attention and love anymore that I used to get and he said he was glad I came to him, that I was special, an amazing kid. He gave me attention like a father should, he said, and now that my father was gone in Vancouver, he was going to help me. I wanted to do the right thing for my mother, didn't I?"

I paused to get my breath, expecting Dave to say something, but he stayed silent.

"It was cool for a while. Really cool. He gave me comic books to read aloud. He watched me play with his GI Joes and stuff. He even got on the floor and played cowboys and Indians with me. I saw him twice a week, and about two or three weeks into it, he told me I was hyperactive and gave my mom a prescription for Ritalin. And then he told my mom to sign me up for karate which I liked, you know. Anyway, about a month into seeing him, I got to feeling like he was my best friend, so I told him about the stomach aches I'd had since the divorce. You know?"

Dave nodded.

"So, he told me to unbuckle my belt and unzip my pants. He was a doctor so he would do a couple tests on my stomach, which would save Mom from having to pay for another doctor. So, I unzipped my pants. I mean, he was a doctor, right? So, I just did what he asked, and he used his hands and pressed under my shirt, on my stomach."

Dave sat up and wrapped his hands around his raised knees, dipping his chin into the tiny space between his knee caps, listening.

"He pushed on different places down there, looking for an ulcer, he said. He couldn't find anything, so he told me to pull my pants down farther. I pulled my pants down but not my underpants. Then he told me to turn over and he pushed and poked on my back and under my underpants, on my ass, like he was looking for something. All the time he was talking about what a cool boy I was, a special boy, a brave boy. I mean, he had charisma, like Burt Reynolds or John Wayne. He had a deep voice, the kind of guy people listen to . . ."

I trailed off for a second but continued.

"The point is, I was a little kid. I just did what he said to do. So, after he felt down under my underwear and couldn't find anything, he goes, 'Pull your underpants down further please,' and there I was lying on my stomach with my little jeans and underpants down at my ankles while he used his hands to find what was wrong with me. Then he said, 'I'm not finding what's wrong yet. Take everything off so I can give you a full physical exam.' He was a doctor, so I took my shoes off, then my pants and my underwear and my shirt. Now I was naked and feeling weird, but he was all nonchalant touching me more than most doctors, especially feeling my privates, like he was weighing the little nuts or something, but the weird thing was, this felt good in a tingling way, like when you beat off, you know? How many times a week you beat off, Dave?"

"Huh?"

"How many times?"

"I don't know. A couple times a week," he murmured.

"No way! What teenage boy only beats off twice a week?"

"Maybe a few more times," he admitted.

"It doesn't matter. I'm just trying to get at why you don't freak out hearing all this—because of what Allen did to you. That's the psychology of it. You'll see in a second that you're not as tainted as me, but still, Allen messed with your privates which messed with your head like Dr. Francis messed with mine. Like in Siddhartha, you know, but without the sex stuff, we're stuck in our 'net of thoughts' and rather than 'finding the Self,' we're trapped in *samsara* and can't get to *atman* or *nirvana* because of the weird stuff in our heads . . . Anyway, what am I talking about? Back to the story. . . so I stripped down like a good little boy and he prodded here and there. He explored all over me. It felt good. I had never beaten off before. I didn't know anything about my privates except to pee."

Dave pulled his body up even tighter, rocking on the hood of the car. He was such a good listener that I just kept on going.

"So, you know what happened? I got a boner. 'Your boner is bigger than most boys' boners,' the doctor said. If he was my dad, he said, he'd be honest and tell me I was gonna become a big, strong man who wouldn't ever be afraid of anything. 'You're a special kid,' he said as he was playing with my nuts." I turned to Dave. "You see how weird my stuff is?"

"Uh huh," he whispered.

Tilting my head back, I heard the words coming out as if I was about six feet away from my own mouth. "The guy talked about 'erections' and 'boners' like it was so normal. 'That's what's causing your stomach aches,' he said. 'It's not your stomach actually, but your groin that's the issue.' I didn't know what 'groin' was. Then he goes, 'Benny, do you want me to show you some magic?'

"Me, the dufus, I go, 'Okay.' I mean, Dave," I turned to him, "you can't understand this part cause you never felt cool with Allen and those guys touching you, but with a guy like Dr. Francis, you feel cool. I felt like I was gonna be a big brave man and getting a boner with him was cool, really cool, like finally I was gonna learn the stuff a man knows, like regarding this special thing I have . . .

"Is this too weird?" I asked, suddenly self-conscious.

"No way," he assured me, his voice whispery but certain.

It would have been difficult to stop talking even if he hadn't encouraged me. It was like I had opened up a box and couldn't close it, didn't want to close it, desperately wanted to tell someone about this so I could get it out of my head.

"Anyway, we got down on the floor, and he pointed and said, 'This is your groin.' He took hold of me with his hand and said, 'Here's how you release the pain. It will seem weird at first, but don't worry, it's okay.' Right there, he showed me how to beat off with his hands on me, then he told me to do it myself while he watched. I did it with my hand and then suddenly I whined, 'I'm gonna pee!' but he smiled and said, 'No you're not, this is something else.' But I was scared and he groked how scared I was, so he scooped me up and carried me to the bathroom in his office. No piss came out, but man I thought I was gonna pee, I really did. He just stood with me at the toilet, saying it was safe now to keep doing what I had been doing with my hand."

Dave unraveled his arms from around his legs and lay back down on the car hood shoving his hands between his legs, at his groin, like he was cold.

"Anyway, that's my story. I exploded in the bathroom like a geyser all over myself, and it was the most amazing feeling. I mean, it's true, right. The first time is weird, but you feel something pretty cool, I gotta admit. So, then Dr. Francis says, 'I am so proud of you, Benny.' And he was so cool and nice.

"See, that's what's so confusing. This guy wasn't a bully like Allen. He was so nice. He wiped my cum off with Kleenex and put the wet Kleenex to my nose. He wanted me to smell it! But he was a doctor, right? I didn't know what was going on. I just felt good and proud. You know?"

I turned to Dave. "You grok it, right? If I was a gay guy, it would be okay, him playing with me like that, but I'm not gay, and I don't understand it. You know what I mean?"

"Yeah," he said.

He was listening very intensely, surprised but not judgmental. It was almost like he was adding it up in his head like a math problem or like he was calculating a chess move, his whole face and forehead and eyes concentrated on getting it just right.

"When Judith came back to the office and got me, I wasn't confused yet. I was happy. All that night at home she said I was in a good mood, maybe the therapy was helping.

"'Yeah,' I told her. 'I'm working on not becoming angry or violent anymore.'

"She said this sounded very mature to her and we were both so glad I had Dr. Francis to help me. After that she kept taking me back to Dr. Francis twice a week and I seemed to be getting better. My counselor at school thought I was better. But I couldn't tell anyone about this doctor making me cum with his hands, right?"

I paused and asked Dave, "You freaking out, man? Is this too freaky?"

"No," he whispered. "What else happened?"

"Don't freak out, man."

"I'm just listening."

*Get everything out*, I thought to myself. *Get everything out of your head.* But I asked, "When was the first time you beat off, Dave? I bet it wasn't with some guy in an office."

He answered quickly like he expected the question to come at some point. "I was fourteen. I looked at a Playboy."

"Really, fourteen?" I didn't know a boy who didn't beat off till fourteen, but then with Dave being so physically undeveloped, maybe he just didn't get the urge to start until then.

"Maybe you were lucky in a way," I figured. "You didn't get into all this head-tripping masturbation and sex stuff till later. And it's lucky your worst stuff with Allen happened when you were basically sixteen. My stuff happened when I was ten which is pretty young. I think Dr. Francis messed with my psychology of the Self and all that. Hey, you okay?"

Dave seemed to be trembling in the dark.

"I'm fine," he said, his whispering voice giving way to a louder tone. "Keep going."

"The fact that you don't think I'm weird is weird too, right. You and I are a couple of freaks. We're not part of the normal 'growing up' plan. Like, I had a *bar mitzvah*, and that was supposed to be my growing up, right? Then I got my driver's license and I first had sex with a cute girl . . ." I sped quickly through that lie. "I mean, I'm basically supposed to be a man by now, right? So, do I really have any proof Dr. Francis hurt me? I mean, maybe I'm fine. I mean, I sweat naked with Eagleclaw and the guys at the Rez, and I'm in locker rooms all the time with naked guys and I don't freak out. I'm nervous all the time, yeah, but I think I'm pretty normal . . ."

I trailed off, not sure what I should say next and not wanting to give Dave the other details of what Dr. Francis had made me do.

I felt happy, or some feeling like it, now that I had talked and not been hated by Dave.

"Was that all you and the doctor did?" Dave asked, as if he saw into my head.

"Kind of," I quickly lied again. "We just beat me off a lot, then Dr. Francis took his clothes off. He was hairy! I'd only seen Harvey naked, so I started freaking out and Dr. Francis got on the floor and told me to watch him beat off. I mean, his nuts and his . . . thing were huge! But anyway, what's the denouement of all this? The denouement is, I got out of there after the second time he beat off in front of me. I mean, his cum was like a fountain compared to mine and it got all into his thick brown pubes and I got a nervous stomach when he made me wipe it off him with a

Kleenex. It was scary, like my soul was telling my Self, 'Dude, this is not good.' Like when Allen tied the shoelace on you. You knew that was way weird, right?"

"Yeah."

"When Judith picked me up that day, I told her I wasn't gonna go back there. I was gonna be a perfect good boy. I learned my lesson and I told her to save her money. I was good now. Two months of paying Dr. Francis was enough. She looked at me really carefully and then said she was okay with that if we made a bargain: I had to be good all week, do all my chores, not get mad at her or anyone—if I did that, I didn't have to go back."

I stopped talking and looked at the night sky and felt in a weird way like I had never really looked at it before. I stared at the big dipper and the moon but was really remembering what I couldn't tell Dave—how I went to that office for months, sucked on Dr. Francis' huge penis, scared of it, crying, how he sucked on mine, how he said he would send me to a mental hospital if I stopped sucking on him or if I ever told anybody or if I refused to do the thing next week that would make us like one body and one mind forever.

"It's going to be inside your ass," he said. "You're a troubled boy, and I'm a doctor, and I know you'll like it, and remember, no one will believe you if you tell our secret, but they'll believe me when I say you're making things up. You ever seen a mental hospital? They're worse than prisons."

"I was lucky to escape, man," I said to Dave, finishing the story before I accidentally told him all the other details. "Judith canceled my next appointment with him, and I stayed a really good boy after that, believe me. It was like he cured me. When he called my mom and asked where I was, she said I seemed a lot better and that she couldn't afford the therapy anymore, and I stayed a really good boy and never went back to him. I mean, that's strange, if you think about it. I got into so much weirdness with that doctor, and it should have made me a bad person, I guess, right? I mean, my mom says if you are abused, you 'continue the cycle,' but it didn't make me bad. It made me a very good boy. And I figured some stuff out, like don't be too rebellious so you do bad things that will lead to police and then psychiatrists.

"Anyway, that's the story of little Benny and his psychiatrist, and that's why I'm gonna help you do something to Allen. I've gotta stop being so afraid of what's not even right in front of me but only in my head. Whoa, check it out," I pointed to a firefly that came right up to Dave's feet. "That's spiritual, man. That could be your sacred power animal or something."

"Yeah, sure, that's a good sign," he said as the firefly flew back into the field. "*Rara avis*. That means rare bird."

I was right to tell Dave, I told myself. It would take some of the crap out of my head, and I didn't have to tell him everything because helping him punish Allen would get everything out of my head once and for all. I closed my eyes and pictured Allen Tremmel at the back of his father's store, loading furniture into trucks. Watching him from across the street I had thought how Siddhartha and Eagleclaw would never hurt a boy in the way Dave wanted to hurt Allen, but Siddhartha and Eagleclaw didn't have to cleanse themselves of thoughts that were always scary. Siddhartha was never scared.

Wasn't that the problem with books and movies and plays? The characters hardly ever seemed scared except if they fought a war or a villain, and when they were scared, the villain was right there, ready to be fought, and the hero always won the fight, even against the shark, unless the play was minimalist and tragic, but that was a different thing. Plus, there were no movies or TV shows or plays that showed what Allen did to Dave or what I did with Dr. Francis.

Wiping at my eyes, I said to Dave, "You and me. Together. We'll convince Allen not to be a bully anymore. We'll change that asshole's whole way of thinking."

I pounded my chest, right above my heart.

"That's got to be the psychology of this, right? This whole summer is meant to be. It's not wrong or evil like our parents would say it is—punishing Allen, I mean. It's just what we have to do. I have to help you, my blood brother, then we'll become normal guys again, not weirdo misfits who think too much inside their heads and are always scared, right?"

"Yeah," Dave nodded, seeming revived now, like my story had made his life easier again. "Fighting back against a bully is crucial. And I need you to help me. That's meant to be. And it's okay, Ben, what you told me. I won't tell."

"I know," I said. I knew he wouldn't.

"Did you ever tell your mom or dad anything about Dr. Francis?" he asked.

I shook my head. "It would kill my mom, man. She kept taking me to the pervert doctor. She'd be toast if she knew she made all that bad stuff happen. I gotta protect her, right? She's my mother."

"Yeah," he said. "Yeah, I grok that. We gotta protect our mothers. I never told my parents about Allen."

"Yeah. I mean, when I decided to be nice to my mom, I knew what it meant. It meant that no matter what, Judith can't ever know."

Dave nodded. "I grok that. The reason I can't tell my mom about Allen is because then she'd think that she's a bad mom, like it was her fault. Moms always think that."

"Yeah," I agreed.

"And there's no way to tell your dad, right?" Dave confirmed. "I mean, if I told my dad about what Allen did to me, he'd just know I'm a wuss and a freak."

"Yeah, dads are complicated," I agreed again.

"But I wish I could get Bert to come watch me punish Allen. He'd respect me as a man, I think. He doesn't respect me at all now. I'm just a pussy kid to him."

"Yeah," I said absently. "You know, every summer with Harvey I wish something would happen so I could tell him everything about Dr. Francis. But nothing does, and that's okay. I mean, until I met you and heard about Allen, I was too scared to really do anything about the stuff inside my head. Like, I talk about liberating the Self and all that, but I didn't really know what I could do." I turned back to him. "Now you've shown me a course of action, Grasshopper. You have shown me the way of the warrior, young David."

"Yeah, the freaky warrior," he chuckled.

"Yeah," I said as I sat up, ready to change the scene.

"Okay, now shake my hand and promise me. Say it out loud. I, David McConnell, promise I'm never going to tell anyone about Dr. Francis."

Dave grabbed my hand with his soft, clammy hand. "I, David McConnell, promise I'm never going to tell anyone about Dr. Francis."

I let go and wiped his sweat off on my jean shorts then jumped off the hood of the car to get my circulation going.

Dave jumped off the car too, saying jokingly, "I wish we could cut Dr. Francis' nuts off. Or Allen's. Or maybe make both of those guys beat off right in front of us. That would be freaky, but that would really punish them."

I thought he'd meant it as a joke, but then thought about his comment a bit more and said, "Wait. Did you really mean that, about making Allen masturbate in front of us?"

"No way," Dave laughed. "I was just trying to make you feel better. We don't have to do that."

I shook my head vehemently. "Man, even if you hit Allen, you can't become an animal or a devil, okay? You gotta stay on the sacred side of things, the good side. Doing really bad things to Allen, even though he's a bully . . . well . . . it would still be like going backward. I don't want to go backward. We have to do the thing that builds the sacred Self, not destroy it. Right?"

"Sure, sacred," Dave nodded enthusiastically. "*Onus probandi, Benjamin.*"

"Yeah, whatever that is, Latin boy. When you do your sweat ceremony with Eagleclaw and the guys, you have to be sacred and protect God and the spiritual balance so that you're, like, protected by the animal spirits and the ancestors. Like, we can't do anything to Allen that our Jewish relatives who died in the concentration camps would think is evil. See what I mean? That's the key."

Dave nodded. "Sure. Absolutely. I grok that, man."

"Put 'er there." I raised my palm and Dave high-fived me a good strong slap and we laughed at the sound.

Then we climbed in the car, and I turned the ignition and clicked on the radio. Grand Funk Railroad sang "We're an American Band" as I accelerated down the gravel road, over the cattle guard, and onto Highway 3. A huge semi-truck whooshed past, and as I pulled the Dart in behind it, the smell of manure filled the car.

"Sorry we can't go get Dr. Francis," Dave said. "That would be cool."

"Whoa, no way, man," I said. "Allen's still kind of a kid, and two kids can mess with another kid, but trying to do something to an adult like Dr. Francis? There's no way."

Dave shrugged and turned the radio dial. "Radar Love" by Golden Earring was playing, and we sang along until the song ended. Dave turned the dial again, and we began singing along to

"Low Spark of High-Heeled Boys" as we glided toward the lights of Durango.

I felt almost ecstatic about having told my secret. Dave had seemed hurt by it, empathic, and normal enough as he listened. That was good. I had been right to tell him.

In the distance, the lights of Durango seemed fake and the outline of the mountains was like a painting for a set in a play at the Rez. The real stuff was back at Dr. Francis' office. The real stuff happened on a planet that was once big but now was only big inside my brain, like it had gotten sucked into the mind of a boy, like Dave's ideas, like everything lived in a kid's mind, huge there, vibrating his muscles and nerves, which felt so weird because a second ago I had been so happy.

The Traffic song ended, and I asked Dave, "You still like me, right? We're still soul mates, right?"

"Of course," Dave laughed. "You're the brave guy now. Your secret is way bigger than mine."

"Yeah, Dr. Francis was scary, but at least he never got close to cornholing me like Allen tried with you and the fishing pole. But I guess Allen did stuff to you with other guys watching so, like, it wasn't private, but . . . I don't know which is worse." I rambled some more until "Stairway to Heaven" came on. It was one of our favorites, and we sang along.

After the song ended, Dave turned the volume down. "I have an idea about how to get Allen to the Lester's barn."

"Okay," I said.

"I don't think we can lure Allen out to the Lester's place by just calling him on the phone and asking him. He might bring friends. We gotta surprise him somehow, so I think you should hide on the back floor of his car in the dark in your KKK outfit, then when he starts his car and drives off, you sit up and put a gun to his head and use your Texas accent to make him drive to the barn."

This was supposed to be Dave's thing—he was supposed to do the hard stuff.

"I think that's the best way," Dave said. "You would be very brave."

\* \* \*

That night I lay in bed picturing myself on the back floor of the Camaro in the darkness. I imagined Allen getting into the front seat in the dark, unaware of me under the blanket he kept on the back seat with his camping equipment. I saw myself rising up after he drove away from the curb with the gun barrel pointing into the side of his head.

Could it work?

Maybe if we unscrewed the light bulb in his overhead light.

No one locked their cars here in Durango.

That was good.

It might work.

I was becoming excited about the risk and thrill of doing it.

Wasn't it true—the more I did, within limits, to Allen, the more I could get Dr. Francis out of my head?

Yes.

Yes.

Falling asleep, I just kept telling myself, Yes.

## Chapter 6

IN THE MORNING, I wrote in my journal.

*I slept better than I have in years because I confessed to Dave, and now I'm finally ready to grow up. Dave and I are going to do something great with our lives. Sometime within the next two weeks, we are going to find the Self in a sacred and heroic way.*

Setting my spiral notebook down, I moved to the bookshelf, pulled down Hermann Hesse's *Siddhartha* and Castaneda's *The Teachings of Don Juan,* and opened them to my favorite dog-eared pages. Lovingly, I read sentences of truth and beauty, then wrote them into my journal feeling like I was Siddhartha just before his enlightenment, just on the edge of it.

*Truly,* I copied, *nothing in the world has occupied my thoughts as much as the Self, this riddle I know nothing about.* No longer would I know nothing about Ben Brickman. No more. *This summer,* I wrote, *I am getting to fully know myself, and I have Dave to thank for that.*

Feeling happiness without any pot in my system, I set my journal aside and opened Castaneda's book to a dog-eared page and read aloud as if to Dave, like we did sometimes, how anyone could be a warrior and a man of knowledge if he just challenged and defeated his enemies. Into my journal I wrote, *When I defeat my enemies, learning will no longer be a terrifying task. I will defeat my enemies and become a man of knowledge.*

Putting my journal away, satisfied, I wondered what Dave was up to. Walking to his house, I found him doing chores. Together, we mowed his lawn and then mine, putting the grass in trash bags, his mother thanking us with iced tea and chatting with us, always looking at me, always seeming to want to take me aside to talk about Dave. I had already come over to the house one day looking for Dave and she forced me to sit down and drink iced tea with her so she could grill me about Dave. I wanted to be nice to her because I knew how silent Dave could be and said good things about her "very good son," and she thanked me for talking with her about him, the Rez, how he played piano out there, how he was not depressed. We promised not to mention to him that she was "checking up on him," but I did the next day, and he said, "I know, that's my mom. She's always worried about me."

"I've got something huge to show you," Dave said after chores. The "something huge" appeared back in my basement—folded pages he pulled out of his pocket for me to read about exactly how we would take our revenge on Allen.

"Cool, man," I smiled, as he showed me what he called his "script."

*"We will drive Allen to Lester's barn where we'll have the place set up already.*

*We'll use the gun to get Allen to take off his clothes and . . ."*

I frowned because he called it a script but wrote it like a story not a script. I opened Pinter's *The Homecoming* to show him how to do it properly.

He practiced right there in front of me, a quick study in everything he did.

*INT. NIGHT. Lester's Barn. Moonlight through open roof. In our white robes, Ben holds Red's gun on Allen, standing ten feet from Allen so Tremmel can't rush him. Using his Texas accent and deep adult voice, Ben speaks.*

*Ben:*
*"Boy, we're gonna punish you for your sins.*
*Take off every stitch of clothing."*

*Tremmel:*
*"No way!"*

*Ben shoots gun into the sawdust right next to Allen's feet, gives the*
*command again.*
*Tremmel strips.*
*Dave enters, picks up two-by-two, hits Tremmel with it.*

"Better," I admired. "See how this form works?"

He saw. From then on, he wrote his ideas down like a play.

The next afternoon Dave and I worked in the basement sewing robes out of white sheets and hoods out of pillow cases. Harvey had taught me how to sew costumes years ago, so I did most of the work using Harvey's old sewing machine. Within a day, we had the costumes ready. My stomach felt queasy about the white KKK robes—but I saw how they could seem to come from a deep concept, a great disguise for a couple Jewish kids. Dave and I got stoned less and worked hard on what we began to call "our sacred mission." Dave found a picture of Catholic robes in a book, and we agreed how "meant to be" it was that except for our pointed white KKK hoods, the white robes themselves looked medieval Catholic. Because he was raised Catholic, Dave said, this association "is so powerful, so . . . immense."

When he stood up straight and lifted his finger in the air like a king or a prophet, the dorkiness of it made me jump on him and wrestle him down until we laughed.

All the time we prepared, Dave seemed puzzled about when to get his father's gun out of the master bedroom closet at home.

It wouldn't be easy because his dad might look for it, and we couldn't keep it for long. The gun had been Red McConnell's, Dave told me, the gun Red had used to shoot himself in the head. This made the hair on the back of my head stand up and gave me goosebumps.

*INT. LESTER'S BARN. NIGHT. Ben points Red's Colt .45, model 1911A1, toward Allen. The gun is silver and brown, with a magazine that holds eight rounds. The gun scares Tremmel.*

I visualized getting Allen to the Lester's barn, making him strip naked, holding a gun on him, shooting it to scare him . . . all this felt too real, too intense, scarier than death. But I hid my feelings and over the next four days, good things also happened. I felt better about Dr. Francis, the images not in my head so much, and I felt less sickened and ashamed about liking some of what we'd done in his office. As Dave and I worked on our sacred mission, I felt more confident, less in need of pot, more certain that the night with Allen would cure me.

But whenever Dave (who read my mind like a best friend could) wanted to revise the script to include me doing more to Allen than holding the gun on him, I refused. I would only hold the gun on Allen so Dave could hit Allen with a stick—we would do nothing more.

"And remember, Dave, you can't hit Tremmel in the head or even on the nuts," I reminded him. "If we hurt Tremmel permanently, he would go to a hospital and the cops could find us somehow and we'll go to jail for life. We gotta be careful, man."

"Okay, right," Dave would say, wheels turning behind his eyes.

"I mean it," I insisted, acting like the big brother, thinking of myself as the man in control of this adventure.

"Okay, okay!"

Dave got annoyed with me for constantly repeating how little I would do, and how little he should do to Allen, but I stuck at it until he finally agreed with me—or so I believed.

All that time a part of me wished we could do more to Allen, get more revenge, and I was so grateful to Dave for not treating me any differently than he did before he knew my secret about Dr. Francis that I hugged him more than a few times during that week. He didn't like to hug, a stiff board with stiff arms, but he let me hug him.

Our only big fright about rehearsals came once with Harvey. Without costumes, while Harvey napped, we rehearsed my crucial part in the back seat of my father's Dart. Something must have woken him because he came out of the house and saw us. Quickly, Dave said, "Hi Harvey. We're just trying to figure out if it's realistic in *Mission Impossible* that people hide in the back seats of cars."

"Very good," he nodded approvingly. "You boys are testing out the verisimilitude, the realism."

"Yeah," we agreed, grinning. "Verisimilitude, for sure."

"Close one," Dave grinned when he went back into the house.

"Yeah." My stomach nauseous, I slapped Dave's shoulder for his quick recovery.

Heading up the street later in the day on our bikes, we started focusing on Tuesday as the night we could get Allen alone *and* have access to the Dart. From our surveillance of him the last two Tuesday nights, we noticed he went bowling with his girlfriend, Melissa, then drove back to her house afterwards. Allen and Melissa always went inside for about an hour, probably having sex, and Allen left his car parked outside on the street, unlocked. On this same night, Harvey played bridge at the Percy's house two blocks away. He liked to walk there, so Dave and I could get the Dart.

"Let's do it next Tuesday," Dave said logically, and I agreed. The plan was good, we had rehearsed everything, we felt good. Spending the next few days going to the Rez, doing our chores, talking with Molly and Harvey as much as we needed to, we wrote out every possible flaw in our plan and saw that if there was a flaw, it would be on my part—chickening out.

*EXT. NIGHT. MELISSA'S STREET. Ben sneaks into Tremmel's Camaro, unscrews the overhead light, and lies down in costume on the backseat floor with the gun. Allen gets in the car and drives away. When Allen has driven a few blocks, Ben rises up.*

*Ben:*
*You done pissed off the wrong people, Tremmel, and the KKK is gonna punish you. Go left and turn west out of town.*

"You gotta be absolutely still in there," Dave reminded me.

"Of course!" I spoke with confidence but practiced in the basement behind the couch, talking myself into being brave enough to lie back there and not move so that when Allen came up to his car in the dark, he wouldn't see me there. I practiced using my Texan accent, speaking like an adult, angry but steady, wanting vengeance. If Allen asked why I was doing this, I would just press the gun harder into his neck while I gave him instructions on getting to the Lester's place.

"I'm not the only guy he's bullied in his life," Dave assured me. "He'll give you lots of names and ask you which one you are. Don't worry. I know this asshole."

For his part, our script had Dave driving the Dart, our getaway car, far from the barn so it couldn't be seen after I got Allen inside. Dave would take the distributor caps out of Allen's Camaro, toss them in the woods, and enter the barn. He would carry a Polaroid camera with him to take a photo of Allen naked and beaten. I had argued against this, but he said logically, "It's part of how I can stop him in the future from doing bad things. You'll be gone but I'll still be here, and I can always threaten him with the Polaroid."

That made some kind of sense, and I did worry there would be repercussions later for Dave after I was gone, so I gave in on the photo idea. Before taking the photo, Dave would pick up the two-by-two, hit Allen in the stomach and maybe the back, and then take the photo and we would get out of there.

"And remember," I warned Dave repeatedly. "Don't talk."

Dave agreed, but said proudly, "Listen to this."

He put his hands on his hips and bent his knees cowboy style, drawling with an overdone Texan accent, "Tremmel, yo gonna git beat bloody. Mark my words, son." His voice, deepened enough to pass for a man, didn't squeak right then.

"Don't get cocky," I objected. "All you need is one squeak, and we're screwed."

"Yeah, yeah."

"Seriously, you gotta be silent, okay? Promise you'll stay with the script!"

"Okay," Dave nodded with his frowning face. "I got it, man."

"And your eyes," I pointed. "We gotta make sure Tremmel doesn't see your eyes. Why didn't we think of that before!" My stomach contracted with nervous pain as I suddenly saw how Dave's unique gold-speckled blue eyes could look to Allen. "Put your hood on," I pointed to the pillow case on the foosball table. He did, and sure enough, his gold-flecked eyes could be seen. I took the hood back and sewed the edges of the eyes tighter so that Allen wouldn't be able to see in—although it also meant that Dave would barely be able to see out.

While I sewed, Dave said, yet again, "You could hit Allen too, you know."

Focused on the clap clap clap of the sewing needle in the machine, I didn't answer, hoping he would shut up but also hoping he wouldn't.

"Think about it, Ben. If you don't hit him at least once, how do you get Dr. Francis out of your head? What if I take the gun from you while you hit him, just once, and think about Dr. Francis so that would make the psychology of it work. If you don't hit him, how can you get Dr. Francis out of your head?" he repeated.

"This is your fight," I said, pulling the new and improved pillow case hood from the sewing machine. "I'm already feeling better just from telling you about Dr. Francis. I don't need to beat someone to feel better. That's maybe who I tried to be when I was a kid, but it's not who I am anymore."

I heard myself lying and felt ashamed of it. A voice inside me was growing, telling me that hitting Allen once would be okay. He was a bully anyway, he wanted to shove a fishing pole inside my friend, he needed to be cured of his evil. What would it hurt if Benny Brickman hit him with the board, just once?

\* \* \*

The next night while my father watched TV, Dave carefully snuck a JC Penney shoebox down into the basement. I watched as he opened the lid and removed something wrapped in a dirty red cloth.

"What is that?" I asked.

He dropped the cloth and revealed a black gun with a silver handle.

My stomach turned over with nervousness and excitement.

"There's no feeling like holding a gun, Ben. You're gonna love it. And it's not loaded, so you can pull the trigger."

I took the gun, which felt heavier in my hand than I thought it would be. I pointed it at the ceiling, squinted to sight it, and squeezed the trigger. My confidence up, I held it with both hands, spread my legs for balance, and aimed it at the wall like I was Jack Lord or Danno from the show *Hawaii 5-0*.

"Cool," I smiled.

Two years before in San Jose, Harvey directed a war play, *Incident at Vichy*, and I held lots of prop guns—rifles, handguns, pistols—but none felt like this.

"Check out what's on the magazine."

Dave pointed at the side of the gun where I could just barely read letters and numbers etched there.

"RM, SP4, 28th?"

"Yeah," Dave said. "That means 28th Infantry, Red McConnell, Specialist 4."

"Cool."

I aimed the gun at my books, record albums, and the phonograph on the shelf against the wall.

"There's some bad news, though," Dave said. "I can't find bullets. I looked all through the closet. Maybe we could get bullets from Eagleclaw's stash."

"No way," I blurted, lowering the gun to my side. "Eagleclaw can't be part of this. What about in your garage? Did you look there? Your dad's gotta have bullets."

"I looked everywhere," Dave said adamantly. Then he returned to Eagleclaw, as I sensed he would. "Eagleclaw's got bullets for a .45, Ben. If we just take a few, he won't notice because he doesn't go hunting till around October. Getting the bullets from Eagleclaw isn't bad. Actually, I think it's meant to be."

"How can you say that?"

"Because after we hurt Allen, I'll be doing my first sweat lodge ceremony with you guys. I'll cleanse my path of the heart in Eagleclaw's sweat lodge, and so he, Eagleclaw, would be part of what made me a man."

The sun glared hot through the window as my stomach clutched with guilt. Including Eagleclaw in this made me feel sick. *You are stupid to even be doing any of this, you dufus! You are going to screw everything up again!* But there was no way I could wimp out, no way. We had to go through with our plan and perform our play, which meant we had to have bullets by Tuesday. And yes, Eagleclaw did have lots of bullets. He wouldn't notice if we took three or four . . .

"Okay, you're right, asshole. We'll get Eagleclaw's bullets."

Right then, a shadow of a thought passed through my brain that I had everything wrong—I was not the big brother in control of this whole thing but really a little brother, and Dave controlled every step of what we did.

Later that day we stole the bullets from Eagleclaw. As I drove away from the reservation, Dave pulled seven bullets out of a little plastic bag he had hidden in his underwear.

"Gross!" I joked.

"Let's use two of them for target practice," he suggested with a grin. "That leaves five, which is just what we need."

The thought of shooting an actual gun with actual bullets filled me with so much excitement I stopped feeling guilt about taking Eagleclaw's "sacred" bullets.

Dave loaded a bullet into the chamber and pointed to the rise of the next hill. "Stop there."

We stopped on the rise and looked around as the wind blew sand at us. There was just desert with some cactus and sage brush. We could see anyone coming for miles either way, but saw no one.

Dave raised the gun to shoot at a cactus fifty feet away. He squinted and fired, his bullet disappearing into the sand. Then he loaded another bullet and gave me the gun.

I aimed at the same cactus and missed, the gun recoiling slightly against my wrist and arm.

"We don't have enough bullets to shoot more," Dave said, pushing the gun into his belt above his groin. "We need at least four for the plan, and one extra just in case."

I computed it in my head. We figured it might take two to four shots into the ground or the air to get Allen to comply with taking all his clothes off and accepting Dave's hits.

We wanted a fifth bullet as a spare since we really didn't know what we were doing.

Back in the car we hid the gun and bullets under the passenger seat and drove back to Durango.

Both Dave and I grinned with an intense thrill and the feeling of great power.

# CHAPTER 7

TUESDAY NIGHT CAME STEAMY like some summer nights did, where the sky wanted to rain but had no clouds. Harvey walked over to the Percy's house to play bridge, and Dave and I smiled at him innocently as he left.

After he left, we carried the costumes in paper bags to the Dart, set them on the back seat, and looked up at the stars and the moon. "There's Orion, there's Cerberus, there's the Big Dipper…" I nervously showed Dave the few constellations I knew and that we could see in the city glow. Dave, who knew many more than me, just nodded patiently, lost in his own thoughts.

Driving away from the house, I waved to Mr. Filmont, our old neighbor who always sat on his porch drinking iced tea, reading the paper, or just looking around at the neighborhood.

We drove the two miles to Melissa's house and saw that Allen's Camaro was parked in the same spot as the last two Tuesdays. Dave and I searched for people looking out their house windows or driving by. Seeing nobody, Dave nervously pulled his KKK robe and hood on. I had mine rolled under my arm—I wouldn't put mine on until I got into Allen's car, just in case some neighbor saw a white-sheeted guy moving between cars in the moonlight.

We high-fived and I got out of the car. Dave slid to the driver's seat, while I walked quickly to Allen's Camaro and crawled inside. With a screwdriver I removed the light cover, then the bulb, and replaced the cover. Slipping my costume on, I lay down on the back floor and scrunched up, waiting.

Soon, just as expected, I heard Allen and Melissa's voices on her front steps.

I scrunched even lower.

My stomach clutched.

Allen's front door opened, and he got in without noticing anything out of the ordinary, his mind distracted by Melissa and the radio which, once he started the car, blared out *"and now from George Jones, 'Once You've Had the Best.'"* As Allen drove away it was clear he sort of knew the chorus because he sang along with 'nothing better once you've had the best' loudly then hummed some words and sang others. Hot from the sheets and hood, the gun clutched tightly in my hand, I stayed as still as I could and tried to keep my breath from sounding like thunder in the car. Counting out ten Mississippi's in my head, I kept talking to myself, 'Do it, do it, don't chicken out.' At twenty Mississippi, ten later than I was supposed to, I finally rose up, threw the camping tarp off me, reached the gun up fast, and pressed it to the right side of Allen's neck.

Shocked, he yelled and swerved but got control.

I pressed the gun hard to his neck so I couldn't mess up.

"You dun some bad things, Allen Tremmel. Tonight is yoa reckonin'. Now drive out Highway one-sixty."

I stayed in character, my Texan accent working perfectly, even though I felt my hand and the gun trembling.

He asked, his own voice scared, "What'd I do? Who are you? I didn't do nuthin'."

Like we had scripted, I pushed the gun into his neck harder and told him to shut up.

Now that the tarp was off me, the wind from his open window cooled me down. Like bullies often were, he was clearly scared, his voice higher-pitched as he referred to the white hood he saw in his rearview mirror.

"You sayin' you're KKK?"

"Shut up!" I bellowed.

At a stoplight, he turned to look at me, and I crushed the gun barrel into his cheek, made him turn back around.

"All you need to know is how pissed off the KKK is at you, boy."

As he tried to figure things out, his teeth moved inside his jaw.

I looked back for a quick second and saw Dave four car-lengths behind us as we left Durango and entered the countryside.

Allen fell silent and drove obediently. "Turn in here," I told him when we got to the Lester's farm. He drove up the long driveway, parked and got out slowly—all as I instructed. "Walk into the barn," I commanded, staying ten feet from him so he couldn't rush me. My face and neck and stomach and groin and every other part of me sweated inside the pillowcase and white sheet, but I was staying perfectly in character.

In the barn, Allen said, "I never did nuthin' to the KKK. Who are you, really?"

"You're talkin'," I hissed. "Your punishment just got worse."

The Dart crunched gravel out of sight as Dave parked in the cottonwood trees. Allen heard it and turned but couldn't see anything.

"Once my brother gets here, we'll proceed," I said as Allen fidgeted and lowered his arms. "Get your hands up above your head!" I hollered.

His eyelids dropped down slightly in angry resistance, but he thought better of doing anything right then and raised his hands.

"What'd I do to the KKK? Just tell me that."

He turned slightly to see Dave coming into the barn in his sheet and hood, Dave who eerily said nothing, just walked to his pre-orchestrated position about ten feet to Allen's left. With his hands raised, Allen's belly button and slight line of hair showed above his silver and turquoise belt buckle.

"I never did nuthin' to you guys. Who're you? Who's this other guy? Man, I never did nuthin'."

"You messed with the wrong guys," I said. "Now you're gonna feel what it's like. Take all your clothes off."

Allen shook his head. "What the hell? No way."

The flashlight I held in my other hand illuminated a round circle on his face, showing his eyes and crew cut hair. Above us, the moonlight shined through the holes in the barn's roof and lit Dave's white robe so that it was glowing.

"Take your clothes off," I repeated.

"I ain't no fag," Allen objected, "and I ain't takin' my clothes off for no fags."

His fists were clenched, but he looked smaller than usual.

"I won't say it again, boy. Take everything off."

My voice stayed steady as I prepared to shoot the gun.

"No way," his defiant voice trembled.

"I'll count to three," I said, still in my accent. "W'in I git ta three, you take off yoa clothes. One. Two. Three."

"No way!" Allen challenged.

I lowered the gun and fired a shot into the sawdust near Allen's right boot. He was startled by the loud gunfire that echoed in the barn as I raised the pistol toward his chest. Allen's hands moved in front of his face in a protective reflex.

"Don't refuse what we say again, boy," I drawled, "or the next bullet goes into your kneecap."

"Okay, okay," Allen hissed. "Jesus!"

"Take your clothes off," I ordered.

"What the hell, man?" Allen whined but didn't comply.

I shot another bullet to the left of his left boot.

He squealed and jumped and got the message, tearing his t-shirt over his head with both hands and saying, "You got the wrong guy, I swear. I don't know what's going on, man, but you got the wrong guy. Tell me what I did. Please."

Watching Allen, I thought some part of him must have known a day like this would come.

"You got thirty seconds to take everything off," I drawled, waving the gun at him. "One Mississippi, two Mississippi, three Mississippi . . ."

I kept counting as he awkwardly hopped around removing his boots and shorts.

At twenty-six Mississippi, he stood in his jockey shorts, his hand cupped over his midsection.

"Everything off," I ordered, pointing the gun right at Allen's underpants.

He stood unresponsive, refusing, and I shot the next bullet.

"Geez, what're you gonna do?" Allen whined, pulling his white jockey shorts down. "Whatever I done, I'm sorry. There's no need to do nuthin' bad."

He knew.

"Hands on your head," I ordered, following the script exactly. "You're gonna git hit, and you ain't gonna fight it."

Allen raised his hands, whining, "I'm sorry, man. What did I do? I've been an asshole a few times, but I've always been fair. Don't hurt me too bad."

I held the gun steady, my stomach churning less now that our script—which was mostly all Dave's plan—was going perfectly. Allen's genitals sat right there to hit, and I sensed Dave wanting to do it. Dave had the two-by-two in both hands, and I saw him push down at his own groin with it, like he had an itch or a hard-on he was trying to conceal.

"Here's how it's gonna be," I said as Dave leaned the two-by-two on his leg and pulled the Polaroid camera out of the right side slit in his sheet where it hung on his belt with a keychain. Taking two steps to the side, he raised a camera and snapped a picture.

"What the hell," Allen spat as he covered his flashed eyes.

Dave's hands were trembling from the adrenalin and nervousness.

"That picture will get shown around town if you do anything else to anyone in the KKK in the future," I said. "Just remember that."

"Oh man," Allen hissed again with some anger, some fear, his brain still trying to figure this out. "Don't do anything bad."

"All right now," I continued, as if not hearing. "First my elder here, then maybe me too, we're gonna have at you with that two-by-two."

What power the gun gave me! It didn't matter what Allen was thinking—I had the gun. I hadn't felt power like this before, not ever, and the "maybe me too" snuck out of me as if I *was* going to do something to Allen after all.

Again, I saw Dave flick his hand at his groin as he made sure the picture that had emerged from the camera wasn't soiled. He set the camera down on the sawdust, picked up the two-by-two, and moved to Allen who looked warily at this "elder" gripping the wood like a baseball bat, ready to swing.

"That you, Lee? What're you gonna do? Who are you? Don't hurt me, please. Don't hurt me too bad."

The fearful whine in this evil bully's quivering voice felt very good.

"Go on," I prompted Dave. "I got him in my sights."

Dave inched forward as I told Allen, "You're gonna take a beating, and it's gonna hurt. If you fight back, I'll shoot you in the knee caps. I won't kill you. I'll just cripple you. You understand, boy?"

"Come on," Allen whined, his way of saying he understood. "Come on." Allen's elbows jutted out from about his ear level as he bent his arms toward the coming hits but kept them raised somewhat as ordered. The blond hairs all over his naked body seemed to shimmer in both the moonlight and flashlight. For a second everything was still, as if maybe Dave would not swing the two-by-two—cicadas sang loudly and my ears rang and my heart pumped fast—and then time started again. Dave swung the two-by-two toward Allen's thighs, Allen jumped, and the board hit his right thigh and his genitals. He screamed, fell to his knees, then curled and moaned into the sawdust.

I wanted to shout at Dave for breaking the script—*you hit him in the nuts!*—but I couldn't say anything, could only hold the gun on screaming, writhing Allen as Dave stepped backwards and grabbed the Polaroid camera on the ground. He flashed another picture—*this picture not in our script!*—then put the camera back onto the ground, and raised the two-by-two again. If anyone ever found these pictures, we would go to prison. *No more pictures,* I wanted to yell.

"You're okay, boy," I said to Allen, though my voice had less resolve in it now.

"Oh man, oh please," Allen moaned, his eyes filling with water. "I'm sorry. Don't do it again."

Any anger or defiance I had seen behind his eyes fell further back now into genuine pain.

"Hands back up!" I commanded, trying to get back to following the script. "One Mississippi, two Mississippi . . ." It seemed like an eternity before I finally shot the next bullet, but when the loud whump came, Allen's body flinched and he got up slowly to his knees, a bloody gash showing on his left thigh. His hands guarded his groin, so I couldn't see if Dave had damaged his genitals.

"You stay on your knees, boy, but you got two more seconds to get your hands above your head."

Allen raised his hands above his head. He was wobbly on his knees, his breath came in pants, and there was a red mark on the left side of his penis, yet some anger returned through tears and lips covered in sawdust. "When I find out who you are, I'm gonna kill you," he hissed.

His conviction scared me, but it did something else too. I saw Dr. Francis's clear, powerful look in his eyes, that look when he told me I had to do what he wanted, or he would send me to a mental asylum. I saw Allen pushing Dave's face into the sand in the lagoon. I felt stupid for refusing to say I would hit Allen during rehearsals. Absolutely, I should hit Allen.

"It's my turn," I said to Dave who seemed to expect this and immediately came over to me so we could trade the two-by-two for the gun and flashlight.

We traded quickly and I moved to Allen and ordered him to get up on his feet with his hands up. He complied as Dave lowered the trajectory of the gun from Allen's face to his groin. I stepped up to Allen, hesitating as he cringed and closed his eyes against the blow that was coming. I raised the piece of wood and started to swing . . .

But I couldn't do it.

Damn it!

I stood there for a few long seconds with the two-by-two lifted like a baseball bat, then stepped away and started moving towards Dave to retrieve the gun.

Dave surprised me by stepping back behind Allen with the gun at his neck.

I felt lost a few feet away, too close, way off script, unsure of what was happening.

My brain froze as Dave ordered me, in a Texan accent and fake deep voice, "Get the camera ready, son." Dave moved the gun down Allen's spine. "Get down on all fours like a dog, Tremmel." Dave's voice did not squeak. He sounded like a man, not a kid.

"What're you doin, brother?" I asked.

"What's going on?" Allen whispered, fighting his tears as he got on his hands and knees, his head trying to see behind him.

"Spread your knees wide, boy," Dave ordered. "Now!"

Allen whimpered and spread his knees as Dave skidded the gun barrel down his spine, toward his private parts. Whimpering, begging, Allen closed his thighs against the metal.

"Get them back open, boy," Dave said. "Or I fire this gun!"

Allen trembled, opened his legs back up. "Please don't do nuthin'. I'm sorry. Whatever I did, I won't do it again."

"Keep your knees apart," Dave ordered, his accent and voice holding steady. I didn't know what to do, standing there, unable to intervene. With the gun pressed into him, Allen stared straight ahead on his hands and knees, his body shuddering in fear.

"Now, jerk off," Dave ordered. Then to me, he said, "Brother, you take a picture when he starts doing it."

I wanted to scream at Dave to stop, but I couldn't risk breaking character and Allen realizing who we were.

But what should I do?

Could I risk Allen getting the upper hand by attacking Dave? Should I run?

Should I leave Dave behind? I'd have to drive back to Durango in a stolen car, Allen's Camaro, since Dave had the keys to the Dart.

No, that didn't work. Dave had taken out the distributor cap to Allen's Camaro.

My mind churned.

"Do it, Tremmel!" Dave commanded in a drawl. "Don't make me give this order twice."

Allen flinched and then slowly used his right hand to find his penis and begin to masturbate.

"Please . . . don't . . . take a picture," Allen begged, his body arched with his effort, his face jutting outward like he was a dog. Trembling, I watched Dave move the gun toward Allen's butt.

"Brother, what are you doing?" I shouted, like I'd suddenly woken up.

"Back off!" Dave shouted back.

I began moving around Allen, and Dave raised the gun up to my face. For a long second, I thought Dave would shoot me, but I grabbed his wrist and wrenched the gun away as Allen moaned, climaxing. I cursed and stepped back three paces so that both Dave and Allen were in the sight of the gun. Once more, Allen fell to the floor in a fetal position to cover his genitals. Dave stepped back from his prey as I kicked the board away.

"We're done here," I said, my voice cracking from adrenalin and fear. Returning to the script, I warned Allen, "If the KKK hears you messin' with anyone anymore, we're gonna spread some pictures around. Now you wait here ten minutes. We'll see you again sometime."

Allen wept on the ground, completely humiliated.

I ran out of the barn holding the gun, leaving Dave behind.

# CHAPTER 8

I JUMPED INTO THE DART and dumped the flashlight and gun on the seat. The keys weren't in the ignition, so I had to wait for Dave who silently passed them to me. I fired the engine, shifted to drive, and peeled the tires in the gravel. As I drove, I tore off my hood while Dave slid the sheet over his head. Between almost breathless pants, I yelled, "What the hell, Dave! Are you crazy? We weren't going to do that other stuff!"

Dave turned on the overhead light so that I could see his zit-covered face shining with sweat. Exuberant and grinning like he'd just won the World Series, he banged his fist on the dashboard. "Ben, we did it!" Pulling his costume off he just kept saying, "We did it! We did it!"

I shivered with adrenalin and nausea and shouted, "No, you screwed up!"

He kept grinning. "You stopped me from doing more, but it's enough for now. Oh yeah."

I slammed on the brakes, wrenched my door open, and made it outside just in time to puke on the grassy shoulder.

Dave laughed, getting out his passenger side, letting out a war whoop. As I wiped at my puke-smelling nose with my sleeve, Dave's face looked shocked by a sudden surprise and vomit exploded from him in a guttural sound.

When we were finished, we both stood bent over, our hands on our knees, staring down at our vomit.

"You suck, Dave!" I hissed.

He used his fingers to blow his nose free of the vomit, then pulled his handkerchief from his back pocket and blew it again. I got back into the car, revving the engine, feeling an urge to drive away without him. He sensed it and jumped in as I gunned the accelerator and turned onto the main road, my hands shaking.

"You overdid it, man!" I shouted.

"No way. We are reborn!" Dave's voice, deeper than six weeks ago, still had not squeaked yet tonight. "We did what we set out to do. We made things happen in this hick town. My partner . . ." he turned to me, grinning, ". . . we did what we set out to do. We found the Self!"

"No!"

Dave couldn't see that he had done animal-sexual-devil things.

He wanted to shove a gun up a kid's ass!

How stupid could I have been not to realize Dave would do something like that?

I drove down the rural road and heard my mother's voice saying what she had said to me when I broke her shadowbox, *"Your whole European family did not die in the camps of Auschwitz and Birkenau so you could do things like this!"*

Allen would be dressed by now, running out of the barn.

Would he somehow pursue us?

Was he right behind us?

How could he be? Dave had taken his distributor cap, and I had his Camaro key in my pocket. But still, instinct or paranoia told me to get off the road, hide in the trees somewhere. Yanking the steering wheel to the right, I turned onto a dirt road, one of the thousands outside this town. Our tires spun on gravel as I hit the accelerator after the turn. In the distance were no house lights, so I drove to a place behind a group of tall trees. When I felt safe behind them, I slammed on the brakes, the car skidding to a stop on the gravel.

"What are you doing?" Dave asked. "Let's stick to the plan. We gotta go to the Hanley place and burn this stuff."

I jumped out of the car, leaned against the front quarter panel, and moaned. Dave got out, came around to my side, crossed his arms, and leaned against the car, waiting for me to speak. When I turned my head away from him, he said, "Sorry I puked."

"You did more than that, asshole," I groaned, my head pounding now with pain and some feeling from the sounds of the gunshots like being squeezed very tight.

"But my voice didn't squeak," he grinned, happy.

"But what if it had, Dave? You screwed up. *We* screwed up."

"Not really. Allen never knew who we were. And anyway, you didn't stop me. You just stood there and watched, so you can't be too mad."

Yes, dammit, yes. I had frozen there, shocked, mesmerized, like I had gone into a trance.

"I could have accidentally killed you, you know," Dave said, his voice analytical. "When you grabbed me, I mean."

I felt more vomit rising, bent to discharge, but nothing came out.

"I think you should have let me do my thing completely," Dave said, his arms crossed. "But I guess it's okay. We probably did enough to get Allen and Dr. Francis out of our heads."

I had only held the gun, right? Dave had done all the bad stuff. And hadn't I stopped Dave from doing too much? Yes, good.

"That was gross, Dave, what you did. And what if I still see Dr. Francis? What if he's right here in my head?" I hit my right temple with my palm. "What was I thinking, going along with you on this?"

"You knew I was gonna do it, Ben. I had to mess with Allen the way he did to me. I just had to, and you must have known that. I kept telling you."

"But making him beat off? Are you crazy? He didn't do that to you!"

"That part was for *you*, not me," Dave said, quicker to calm down than me. "Dr. Francis made you do that in his office, so I made Allen do it. For *you*."

What? I looked at his blue eyes with their gold flecks in the moonlight and looked away quickly. What was he saying? That he was the younger brother trying to help the older brother out? But it wasn't our plan. Looking down at my boots, I searched my mind. Where was Dr. Francis? Was he still in my head?

Not right now, no.

Dave unlocked his arms, stepped away from the car, and looked up at the moon.

"Okay, sure," he said. "Sure, we could have gotten caught, we could have lost the gun, we could have torn our disguises. Anything *coulda* happened. But we didn't panic. We taught Allen a lesson. We wrote our play and performed it. That's the point, Ben. Siddhartha and Govinda got out of their books and their spiritual stuff, and they actually *did* something."

If I could have thrown Dave off a cliff right then, I would have, but I also felt some hope. Could Dave's weirdo stuff with Allen really help me with Dr. Francis? Wasn't the whole reason I agreed to this gross evening with my best friend to get Dr. Francis out of my head? And wasn't it true, for a second now, I didn't see Dr. Francis in my head? I only saw Dave and the fireflies around me. I only saw miles of evergreen trees beyond the miles of undulating grass in Durango's light-glow up in the sky. I heard a creek flow to our left, purling and making its sounds. The Silverton train rumbled along the base of the mountains. The moon, almost full, very white, shined slivers of paper onto grass through the trees.

"Aren't you gonna talk?" Dave asked, ten feet from me. "You always talk."

I stared at the moon and the land and the night and tried to think. Allen had tried to push the fishing pole up Dave's asshole, so that was why Dave had wanted to do that. That must be the psychology of it. Dave was the messed up little brother, but I should be mature. I should have never even let this night happen. I had to hope two things right now—that we didn't get caught, and that this was worth it because I would wake up tomorrow and hear in my head, *Dr. Francis, I'm done with you now! Last night was the grossest, stupidest thing I ever did, but it was great. Now I'm happy.*

"No more thinking. We gotta get to work," I said as I pushed up off the car and reached for the metal door handle. "We gotta get any smells of Allen and the gunfire off the gun. And we gotta burn the costumes like we planned. We gotta follow the script."

"Yeah, absolutely."

"What time is it?"

Dave looked at his watch. "Eleven-twenty. Allen looked at our boots a lot. We gotta get our boots off and burned to a crisp."

Again, worried I would drive away, Dave rushed around to the passenger side while I got in behind the wheel and lifted the gun off the seat. It smelled like charcoal or burnt meat along with Allen's smells of sweat and fear and crotch and butt odor. I leaned out of the car door and grabbed some weeds and grass. My hands shook as I held the gun like a gross object in front of me, wiping its snout with the vegetation.

Dave watched me and said, "You want me to do that while you drive?"

For a second, I thought I couldn't give him the gun because he would kill me. The bizarre thought woke me out of my trance. How paranoid could a guy get?

I handed him the gun and the weeds, started the car, and drove. Dave cleaned the gun with the weeds but wasn't completely satisfied, so he pulled out his white handkerchief to finish.

MICHAEL GURIAN

As we drove back to the main road, I turned on the radio to Pink Floyd's "Money." Dave hummed along, then sang the chorus. I drove us to the entrance of the Hanley's small abandoned barn we had prepared for costume removal and destruction. The song ended, and Dave turned down a commercial for hot air balloon rides.

"Because of the oil embargo, we have our pick of these places," he said as he waved his right arm at the abandoned farms, something he had, for some reason, said many times before.

At the entrance to the Hanley's barn, I turned the car off, balled up my sheet and hood, got out of the car, and tossed the clothing on the fire bed. Dave grabbed his stuff from down by his feet, got the flashlight in his hand, but left the gun behind.

We stood beside the fire bed and Dave put on his overdone Texan drawl. "You'll see, Ben. It's great to have a secret no one else has. We fulfilled our mission, son."

"Let's just get this stuff burned," I muttered.

A bat squeaked above us in the half-empty vault roof of the barn. Moonlight shined through missing roof slats, just like at the Lester's. Dave pointed the flashlight beam at the fire pit we had constructed last week just for tonight, like the one at Eagleclaw's pond, a foot deep, surrounded by a circular rock wall. I pulled my Bic lighter out of my pocket as Dave dumped his stuff in the pit. The sheets landed on the bits of hay and wood we had placed there and the whole pile lit into flames quickly.

As our costumes burned, Dave smiled in a way I rarely saw him smile.

I sat on the ground to pull off my boots and Dave did the same. We both tossed the boots into the fire, sat watching the flames, feeling the heat as the sheets burned up. The boots, however, just sat in the flames, barely burning.

"Throw the camera and pictures in," I ordered. "I don't want to ever be reminded of that."

96

"Sure," he shrugged, surprising me with his acquiescence. He tossed the Polaroid camera pictures into the flames and we watched the camera and paper burn in green, blue, and red flames.

I threw more bits of hay in, making the fire smoke, then flame even more. In the firelight, I saw Dave's face lit up, his forehead furrowed in concentration, his chin resting on his fists, his lips still smiling.

His smile helped me calm down, and the fire made me less angry.

"Geez, Dave, what did we do?" I murmured. "What am I doing in Durango, Colorado?"

I thought about Eagleclaw's play about his son dying in Vietnam. This night was as close to war as I would ever get. Maybe now that I had held a gun and shot it and done something mean and bad to some other guy my age, I could think, *Okay, I've been a soldier, I'm grown up now, I can move on.* If I could just survive this next year of high school, I could go to college and everything would be fine.

Thinking my usual million hidden thoughts, I pictured a white sheet of paper in my mind. I wrote, "Cast of Characters."

*The Weirdo Latin-Talking Kid With A Mean Streak.......Dave McConnell*
*The Pretender Boy Who Fights His Own Demons..............Ben Brickman*
*The Strong Mom Who Doesn't Know Some Stuff...........Judith Brickman*
*The Lonely Housewife Who Loves Her Son................Molly McConnell*
*The Fathers.......................Harvey Brickman and Bert McConnell*
*The Villains......................Allen Tremmel and Dr. William Francis*
*The Indian Man Who Wishes People Can Be Free......Eagleclaw Simpson*

I remembered a story Eagleclaw had told me about how he got his Indian name. "My father was drunk after my vision quest and named me Eagleclaw not Eagle Talon, and it stuck."

My father had never named me anything, really, though he often looked at me and said things like, "You are basically a good kid just trying to survive his parents' mistakes."

Closing my eyes, I saw light from the fire flashing through my eyelids like orange flickers through shadow.

Opening my eyes, I heard myself say, "Dave, I don't know what we did, but if we ever tell anyone, I mean anyone, we're both going to prison. This was not 'the Self.'"

"Yeah it was, but yeah, I know, we gotta be strong. There's gonna be times we'll pity 'poor Allen,'" he said logically, "like I whined to myself when he messed with me, or like you whined when Dr. Francis did stuff to you, but we gotta fight that urge, we gotta be silent. You gotta never talk about this, Mr. Always-Talking Ben Brickman."

"I won't say anything, you dufus." I balled my fist up and punched his left bicep.

"Good, and I won't either," he said patiently, kneading his skin from the pain but not complaining. "I'm the silent type."

"That's true." I held my stomach with my hands. Dave's red acne spots shined. Why had I ever been this kid's friend? Why? Why?

Suddenly, like a shock, tears rose up. I tried to stop them as my chin started to quiver.

"Oh God, I hate my weird thoughts. I'm such a dork," my voice cracked. "The adrenalin is messing with me!" I tried to fight the tears.

"It's okay," Dave said. "Don't cry, man."

My hands rose to my face. Someone sobbed far away from me, but it was my body rocking as Dr. Francis' hairy body and penis and testicles flooded my mind. He wasn't gone from my head! Not at all! And now I was crying in front of another boy.

"We're cool," Dave promised. "It's okay, man. We were

unbe*liev*able. We're the strong ones. What're we gonna do for an encore? Get me laid? That'd be an encore."

I laughed through my sobs.

"See," he laughed. "You're okay."

I wiped my eyes with my fingers, sucked a sluice of phlegm inward through my nostrils, felt it in my throat, and swallowed.

"You're just crying cause of adrenalin," Dave confirmed, giving me a way back to my pride. "You got freaked from me doing more to Allen than we planned, and the adrenalin got you."

"Yeah," I nodded, wiping the tears. "Yeah. Okay."

Dave talked for a while about how great we had been, but I interrupted him.

"Dave, we gotta get back home."

I had to move, or I would cry more. I stood up and so did he. Fighting the urge to punch him in the face, I breathed in and out, panting, regretting my tears like a boy always regrets his tears.

"Let's bury the boots," Dave said as he gestured to the boots that were barely burned in the fire circle. "They're gonna take an hour to burn."

"Sorry I cried," I said.

"No big deal, man. Let's bury the boots in one of the old horse stalls."

Instead of dwelling on my crying, he tossed dirt into the fire so it would die down and moved to the back of a wood-rotting horse stall. Following him, I helped dig holes with our fingers in the northeast corner. When the holes were about eight inches deep and twenty inches wide, we went back for the boots. Carrying them with small two-by-twos as pincers, we dropped them into the holes. Smoke rose from them and we dumped dirt on top, smoothing everything, then putting straw over the dirt. By the time we completed the burial of the boots, my adrenalin, my tears, all my emotions were gone.

I just felt empty.

As we left the barn, Dave said, "We gotta have a new pact, man, that we don't talk about tonight, about Allen, about what we did." He held out his right hand, waiting to shake. "Let's say, I swear I will never tell anyone about Allen Tremmel and what we did to him. You are my brother, and I will never betray you."

I agreed and we shook, his handshake stronger tonight than it felt even a few days ago. He recited the line, and then I did, adding, "And we won't talk about Ben's crying."

"And we won't talk about Ben's crying," Dave nodded, shaking my hand again to make the addition official. "So that neither of us will break this pact, let's cut our hands and mix our blood."

It felt almost like déjà vu, like Huck Finn and Tom Sawyer, like the first day I met him and saw his scar. Frozen, I watched him pull out his swiss army knife from his pants pocket and cut his hand slightly. He handed the knife to me, and I did the same. When we finished shaking hands, we pulled back and saw blood matted on our palms.

"It's a pact," Dave said.

"It's a pact," I agreed, wiping the blood into both my hands now as Dave did the same.

How could a kid grow up so much in one night? He seemed to have gone from a brilliant geeky kid to a confident adult in a few hours. As we got to the car, I took the gun out from the back seat and brought it to my nose. Dave saw that I could still smell a little bit of something on the gun, even with my nose stuffed from crying.

"I'll finish it," Dave said, holding out his handkerchief

I handed him the gun and turned on the ignition. Cream's "Layla" played on the radio. The piano and guitar music filled the car as I drove. Dave wiped the gun carefully with his white handkerchief, and I remembered his mother ironing handkerchiefs for him on her ironing board that dropped down from the wall of the kitchen. Still not satisfied with his work, Dave opened the glove compartment to get one of Harvey's pencils. He wrapped the handkerchief around the eraser end of the pencil and shoved it into the barrel of the gun.

When he finished cleaning the gun barrel, he brought the handkerchief to his nose and said, "This handkerchief stinks." He frowned, thought for a moment, and then tossed the handkerchief out the window.

In the rearview mirror, I saw it flash with moonlight, like a white cap on the ocean.

Then it vanished into the thistle and grass along the highway.

# CHAPTER 9

THE SUN SHINED ABOVE US, and the blue sky spread each direction completely cloudless as Dave and I drove to Eagleclaw's land. It was the next Monday, almost a week later. My stomach had been constantly nauseous, my brain constantly working to justify what we had done. My soul was sullen and sad, my eyes turning away from Dave who seemed happy, his pale hands clasped on his lap.

I had been asleep in some way, I decided, and in my sleep, I created a nightmare with Dave as a Fantasarian, but now I had woken up and it made me sick to be awake. For the last week, I had tried talking to Dave about everything, but we weren't friends now like we used to be.

"Are you and Dave okay?" Harvey had asked. "You guys have a fight?"

"We're not married, for God's sake," I grunted.

"You're more silent with each other," he observed, but didn't press me.

At the gym, Dave mainly watched us rehearse, then we took a drive and Pink Floyd played on the radio again. We sang, "*The lunatic is in my head*," and "*There's someone in my head and it's not me.*" When the song ended, I asked Dave, "Do you still have bad stuff from Allen in your head?"

"Nope," he answered immediately. "I feel great."

I looked over at his acne and weird eyes.

"So, hurting Allen in the way he hurt you took what he did to you out of your head?"

Dave nodded. "Allen's got broken ribs. He's the ninety-pound weakling now. I feel good and you should too."

I gazed at a rock formation across the sand and sagebrush and then pulled over to the side of the road, flipped a U turn, and drove back to the gym.

"I can't go to Eagleclaw's right now," I frowned.

Dave didn't ask why, just stayed silent, knowing my thoughts because I had already told him that all the previous bad stuff from Dr. Francis was still in my head. And now the night with Allen filled my head too, like another bad dream I couldn't get free of while Dave, a free man, soared and insisted we were righteous.

"I'm gonna do sweat ceremonies every day Eagleclaw lets me," I said. "I gotta cleanse my soul, man. I'm messed up."

This seemed to contradict what I had just said about going to Eagleclaw's, but he didn't sweat on Mondays anyway, and I couldn't face him today.

Dave shook his head at me and wagged his finger like a parent. "You should stop being so hard on yourself, Ben. We did things right. No one's messed up. You're cool."

"I don't know," I murmured. "I don't know."

"Don't cave in, man. Be strong."

"I'm not caving," I said defensively. "No way."

But if I was really a good friend to Dave, shouldn't I think he was just covering up his feelings and help him get them out? My mom would say, "He's probably feeling bad and covering it up. Help him!" But no, that couldn't be. He didn't seem more damaged than me. He didn't seem to have a lot of feelings. I was the wuss. I was the freaked-out kid.

"Let's go back to the Lester's barn tonight," Dave suggested, seeing my anguish. "Maybe that would make you feel better."

Now who was thinking like the psychologist? Everything had turned around between us. And I wasn't sure going to the Lester's barn would help, but I kind of saw his "get back up on the horse" logic.

That night, after Harvey went to a ballet performance at Ft. Lewis College up on the hill, we got onto our bikes and rode out of town. Pedaling behind Dave, watching his long gangly arms covered in his long shirt, I wanted to be back in New York, far away from him and Durango. I got this feeling every summer near the last few weeks of my time with my father, when I started wanting to get back home to New York. This time, though, I felt a scary, weird, grimy edge to the feeling, like I might be trapped with Dave McConnell forever.

At the barn we lay our bikes down on the dirt and walked into this place we had used last Tuesday for our sick adventure. We sat down in the sawdust and crossed our legs, and I told Dave that he must feel good because Allen was his enemy, not mine.

"I must not feel good because I didn't hurt Dr. Francis like you hurt Allen," I tried to analyze. "That's gotta be it, right?"

"Maybe that's right," he said, still not admitting there was anything bad about what he had made Allen do. "I don't think you know what's really going on, though. I think we're kids who did a great thing. We fought against evil and won. Allen's not gonna bully us or anybody for a long time. That's that. End of story."

I shook my head, unsure but silent. Dave stared at me with cold eyes and said, "And Ben, you better not tell anybody."

The next day at lunch, we drove all the way to Eagleclaw's place. The screen door shut loudly behind Eagleclaw as he ambled toward Dave and me down by the pond where we munched on Lay's potato chips. Dave sat in one of Eagleclaw's old plastic chairs while I swam in the pond, cooling off. A few feet from Dave, Eagleclaw carried three little glass bottles of herbs in his hands. He wore his frayed black gym shorts, his thick black glasses down his nose from sweating in the heat. As he bent down onto his scrawny knees and moved on all fours into the domed sweat lodge, my brain flashed to Allen on the barn floor, naked and on all fours like a dog, Dave running the gun down his spine . . .

Yuck!

I dove underwater to cleanse myself of the thought, then came up, wiped my eyes, and floated as I watched Eagleclaw crawl back out of the lodge with a small bottle of sage. His lodge looked so much like Dave's fort. It was made of bent cedar boughs with quilts, blankets, tarps and a flap for the door which, now, lay on the roof of the lodge like a tongue. Eagleclaw went over to a rack of larger jars on a table in the wooden shade shelter built next to the lodge and, with his long delicate brown fingers, put pieces of dried sage into another jar.

I watched him work, remembering the tobacco, sage, anise, and cinnamon he threw onto the red-hot rocks at the beginning of each round of the sweat ceremony. I loved the aromas from the herbs on the hot rocks as they sparkled like tiny red stars. Early in the summer I asked Eagleclaw if any of his herbs were peyote, and he smiled and said, "I'm sorry, Ben. I am not Don Juan and you are not Carlos Castaneda. There is no peyote for us today."

He finished his work, went back to bend down into the lodge, placed the bottle in the rack next to the rock pit inside the lodge door, then came back out and reached both his hands back behind him to push his massaging fingers into his painful lower spine. I waved to him, but he was focused on his spine, constantly praying for help from Grandfather and the healing spirits for his "lower lumbar disintegration."

Getting all the relief he could from his own hands, Eagleclaw sat next to Dave on the second plastic chair. He patted Dave's arm, and as I floated closer, I watched Eagleclaw point toward the sweat lodge. No doubt he was explaining something about the "spirits" to Dave, how the sweat lodge ceremony would work when Dave and I and some Indians sweated next Saturday.

Dave nodded and murmured something as I stepped out of the water and dried myself with a ragged towel.

"Are you boys hungry?" Eagleclaw asked.

We both said yes, and Eagleclaw asked Dave to go to the house and make some peanut butter sandwiches.

"Sure," Dave agreed, asking us, "You guys want one or two?"

"Two," I said.

"I will eat only one sandwich," Eagleclaw said, lifting one finger.

Dave walked up toward the house, his monkey arms swinging, his long legs loping away from us in his jeans and white socks and sneakers. He didn't care anymore that he looked dorky again. Hurting Allen had made him feel "comfortable to be who he is." That phrase of my mom's echoed with my other thoughts about him, but I couldn't see much more as I sat down next to Eagleclaw and rubbed the goosebumps along my arms.

"That was a great swim," I said. "Mother Earth is great today. Turtle Island is just perfect."

Eagleclaw nodded without emotion as he lit a cigarette and crossed his bony brown legs so that his raised right foot bobbed just off his knee. Raising my own right leg over my knee, I saw blood pulsing in my foot, making my toes bob up and down as birds flew over the west end of the pond toward a high crop of rocks.

"Dave makes good sandwiches," Eagleclaw said, watching the birds.

"Yeah," I said, trying to be enthusiastic. "Definitely."

"I just talked with Dave," Eagleclaw said, letting smoke out of his pursed lips. "He seems happier this last week than usual, but in his heart, he is not singing. Do you know why he is always in such pain?"

"He's not in pain," I corrected. Just the opposite, I wanted to say. "He's just a shy kid. But if he seems happier these days, I think it's because he's excited about doing a sweat with us."

"Is that it?" He turned to me briefly, then back to the pond.

*If anyone's screwed-up, it's me,* I wanted to say.

Eagleclaw lowered his right hand to his knee, his cigarette jutting out from between knuckles almost white in comparison to the brown of the rest of his fingers.

"Dave needs a friend like you, Ben. He is a boy who has many visions but does not know how to talk about them. I was like that as a boy." Eagleclaw turned again to me. "I asked Dave if he could talk to his father about his visions, but he said he could not. I am hoping he will speak with the spirits of his ancestors in the sweat lodge."

"For sure," I agreed.

"I regret abandoning my father for all the years when I would not speak with him. He was an alcoholic and a drug addict, and I despised him—but still, this was a mistake. Boys should talk with their fathers."

"Yeah, for sure," I agreed again, looking into Eagleclaw's thick glasses, seeing his magnified black eyes. "I talk to my father," I said, a half-truth.

Eagleclaw looked back at me, right into my eyes, and I turned away.

"Ben, you have lost that Brickman energy we Indians on the Rez enjoy. Even in the sweat lodge, you are not yourself. What is wrong, Ben?"

"Nothing's wrong," I shrugged, staring at the sun shimmering in a long row of silver waves on the pond. "Just adolescence, I guess. Hormones, you know."

Eagleclaw waited with a big hole of silence I felt like I was supposed to fill. "Or maybe I'm kind of homesick," I said, turning to him so he could look into my eyes and see my honesty. "I mean, I never thought I'd want the school year to start. You know, boring senior year and all, but I guess I do. And I miss New York. I mean, like, coming out here and doing sweats with you . . . that's the coolest thing about this summer . . . but you know, I'm really from New York."

"I understand."

"Hey," I grinned. "Do you get it? Sweating is the coolest thing. I made a pun."

"And what about your friendship with Dave? That is cool too," he suggested, not responding to the joke.

"Sure, yeah, of course. But it's tough moving around to new towns every summer, making new friends, you know?"

Eagleclaw lifted his cigarette to his mouth again and sat back, pensive. "Dave McConnell needs your friendship." He sucked on the cigarette so that his cheeks became brown dents and then let the smoke out in a little cloud. "Dave will benefit from the sweat ceremony. I am surprised it has taken him this long to decide to join us in the lodge. Dave needs to open himself to the path of the heart. He and you both need to get out of your heads, as you like to say, Ben."

"Yeah, that's for sure," I said, glancing quickly at him, as if he knew everything.

"It is good Dave will have his more experienced white friend Ben Brickman in the lodge with him. I am inviting other Indian boys who will be polite to white boys, but these Indian boys will not be Dave's friend. Dave is not an easy friend to have. I can see that."

"He's a quirky guy, for sure," I said.

"You and your friend Dave have many questions these days," Eagleclaw sighed. "But you do not ask them. Have you spoken to your father about what bothers you?"

"Nothing's bothering me, man."

"Yes, it is," Eagleclaw said frankly. "Your thoughts are heavy. This is obvious to everyone but you."

Looking at his yellowing toenails and brown feet and calves, I wanted to tell him everything—*yes, yes, do it, yes*—but I couldn't.

"I guess there is one thought I'm having," I said, trying to make him feel better. "I've been thinking about this thing a lot lately, this koan I learned a couple years ago. You know what that is, right?"

He nodded. "Yes, Ben, I know what a koan is."

"Okay, sorry. I mean, I didn't *learn* this thing. See, that's the problem. My karate *sensei* wanted to teach us something deep, I guess, and he said, 'What's the sound of water in a cage?' I thought, maybe it's like the sound of one hand clapping, right? But no, I knew he meant something else, so I tried lots of thoughts in my head with so many meanings, but I can't really get it beyond the obvious. Like, it's something I think about a lot. Like, it bugs me, you know?"

He looked at me again, waiting for something like the truth to come out of my mouth.

"See," I continued, floundering, "It's like there's the water that could leak out of the cage, which could be a sound of water dripping from the cage, like 'the way of the Tao or Grandfather is the way of water on rock,' or it could make no sound at all if the cage has no leaks, unless you touch it, then it could slosh around. Or maybe it's symbolic, like the water is symbolic of a bird caged in there. You know? Like a bird in a cage?"

He lowered his head, his eyes looking away from mine.

"Anyway, getting an answer to that is something I've been thinking about lately," I smiled. "Maybe that's been occupying my consciousness, you know? What the heck is the sound of water in a cage?"

Eagleclaw sucked in a disappointed breath. "The sound of water in a cage?" he repeated. "What does your father say of this?"

"I asked Harvey last year, and he said, 'Maybe the sound of water in a cage is like a baby growing in the womb.' He was like Freudian and all that, but I prefer Jung's theories to Freud's, even though Harvey is smart, so maybe he's right."

"Ben," Eagleclaw frowned. "Why do you call your father by his first name?"

"You know, that's the way we do it," I shrugged. "He left his family, so I got used to being without a dad. Anyway, he doesn't care."

Eagleclaw shook his head. "A man is lucky to have a father who loves him. This same father is lucky to have a son who loves him. When you disrespect your father, you disrespect your ancestors."

"Geez, man. I feel like *I'm* in a cage," I sighed cleverly. "Look, Harvey doesn't mind me calling him by his first name, so why should you?"

Hearing my harsh tone, I quickly added, "Anyway, I'm thinking about good and evil and big things like that. I'm trying to grok the whole world, you know? The little details like someone's name aren't that important."

Eagleclaw left my words hanging in silence and looked out at the pond, puffing his cigarette once, then twice, then three times. Time passed again in silence, and I got nervous.

Finally, Eagleclaw said, "I think today is not the day for the truth. I hope in the lodge you will find more of the truth."

When Dave returned with our sandwiches, I ate mine away from Eagleclaw and Dave, near the water's edge, almost more sickened by being such a dufus jerk with Eagleclaw than anything else. Maybe I should never sweat again, I thought. Maybe I should just run away right now, run back to New York early. No, no, my parents would freak out and I'd have to explain things, which I couldn't do because of the pact and because I had done so many bad things. No, I had to live out the rest of the summer, just two weeks left, and I had to do the sweat with Dave.

# CHAPTER 10

THAT SATURDAY, Dave and I drove out to the Rez again for the sweat ceremony. He said that he wasn't nervous at all, and he didn't seem to be. He reminded me not to break our pact, acting like he was completely in control.

Still trying to be the big brother, I said, "You're brave to be down to just a bathing suit and zits with all those other naked guys," encouraging with a tone that made the comment both a congratulation and a put down. But Dave didn't rise to the bait.

"Don't worry, I'm not scared of that stuff anymore," he shrugged.

We were silent as we drove the rural roads toward the reservation. I turned on the radio so we didn't have to feel so awkward in our silence, and Lynyrd Skynyrd sang "Free Bird" as if talking only to us. Dave joined me in singing out into the open hot air about how, if I stayed here with you girl, things just couldn't be the same. I will not stay here, I thought. I will get out of here and be free as a bird.

When we got to Eagleclaw's, we met the other guys we would sweat with—all Indian teenagers between fourteen and eighteen, most of whom I knew from the rehearsals or other sweats. Dave had by far the whitest skin in the group, the only guy with blue eyes. I had briefed Dave on how things worked, and everyone knew the drill, filling water jugs for drinking water up at the house, then heading down to the lodge, most of the guys silent with Dave. No one minded starting early to avoid the heat, even though it already felt like ninety degrees as we stood around the fire pit with the rocks inside warming in the flames.

"You must drink a lot of water, Dave," Eagleclaw warned, and Dave promised he would.

In my fifteen sweats so far this summer, I noticed the native guys didn't seem to need as much water as me or Harvey, and they needled me about it.

Eagleclaw pointed to our wrists, and Dave and I and a few others took off our watches and stowed them with our clothes in the shelter next to the lodge. Once we all gathered back together, Eagleclaw and the Indian boys did their prayers in the Ute, Lakota, and Navajo languages, then Eagleclaw asked everyone, "What good deed have you done in this last week?"

I blinked my eyes shut for a second. Eagleclaw always began sweats with this question, but surely today he directed it to Dave and me. The Indian boys began by giving very short answers. One boy said he helped his parents with something. Another boy said he taught math to his little sister.

When it was Dave's turn, he said, "I visited an old man who was dying."

I said, "I helped my father with the plays."

The sweat ceremony hadn't officially begun yet, so all of us were bare-chested but still dressed in swim trunks or jeans. Two of the boys were fatter than the rest of us, with huge brown arms and legs and stomachs and flabby breasts. Their Christian names were Rick and Bill, but their medicine names were Hawk Seeking Blood from the Sky and Heart like Lightening in the Winter. I had sweated with them before, but we rarely spoke.

John Torrance, whose Indian name was Fast Otter, stood to Eagleclaw's right, his assistant for these sweats—a guy in his twenties. He taught fifth grade at the Indian school on the Rez and smoked a lot of cigarettes.

Looking at skinny, shirtless, almost-albino Dave, I thought, *his medicine name will be Weirdo Dave.* But then I felt bad for thinking that because now it seemed like taking off his white undershirt and long sleeve plaid shirt made him more nervous than he expected to be, almost weirdly scared, like he had to keep his hands from shaking by crossing his chest with them. Something had changed in Dave this last half hour or so.

Eagleclaw directed us to hold hands and join in another Indian prayer, which he had taught me before in English. While the other boys recited the prayer in their languages, in my head I said:

*Mother Earth, you love us.*
*Father Sky, you protect us.*
*Six Directions, you hold us.*
*Seventh Direction, you lead us.*

When the prayer was finished, Eagleclaw reached into a pouch on his waist, pinched some tobacco, and sprinkled it onto the fire which fizzled and burned, giving off the sweet, pungent and familiar smell of tobacco smoke. Meanwhile, Fast Otter walked around the circle in front of each of us holding a stalk of lit sweet grass. Smoke rose from the stalk as each of us motioned the smoke with our hands into and around our faces and chests, smudging ourselves, while we were supposed to say a silent prayer, inviting the Great Spirit into us. It was almost exactly like what we did when my family would go to *shul* on Friday nights, waving the Sabbath candle light into our eyes and faces and chests three times.

*Grandfather, Great Spirit, Oh Lord,* I prayed silently, my hands moving, *Please cleanse my soul and let today be the day I get everything bad and evil out of my head.*

Fast Otter brought the sweet grass to Dave who had watched everyone else's gestures and did just what we did, closing his eyes, saying some inward prayer I could not discern as he brought the smoke to his zitty face and black-head chest. After he smudged himself with the smoke, he moved his hands back down to the crotch of his blue swim shorts, clasping them together there.

Fast Otter lay the burnt braid of sweet grass in the dirt as Eagleclaw said a prayer to all the directions—East, South, West, North, Up, Down, and Within—turning his body in four-square and rocking it up and down, then touching his head and his heart. When he was done, he said in English, for Dave's benefit, "*Hojo nanado* is with us today, the healing spirit of my brothers from the west." By brothers to the west, he meant Dave and me, but also the Navajo tribe to the west because "hojo nanado," I knew, was a Navajo term.

Dave couldn't chant any of the things the other Indians could, but I could chant a little bit from experience. When I didn't know the Indian words, I hummed along because Eagleclaw told me early in the summer that it was okay to do that. In fact, he said, it was a way of "helping the spirits come to us." Dave didn't chant or hum, but when we turned to face a certain direction as Eagleclaw had, he tried to imitate us, embarrassed by his poor timing. When we stood again and faced the fire, our foreheads and arms and chests beading with sweat, Dave's body seemed to get even redder because the heat and the sweat seemed to swell some of his zits.

He looked nervous, uncomfortable, fidgety, not at all like the confident guy in the car. His eyes remained downward, never rising to look anyone in the eyes. I thought right then—a premonition, maybe—that I should suggest to Eagleclaw that he go up to the house and not sweat with us. But then I thought about what he had made Allen do and decided that his weird ideas needed cleansing for sure, so I turned away from him as Eagleclaw began his next ritual—dancing around the fire pit. All of us followed him in a round dance, Dave trying awkwardly to learn the footwork. I felt both happy and disappointed to see Dave, unable to get the footwork, step out of the dancing circle.

When the dance finished, the rest of us stood still again, and Dave returned to his place in the circle with us. Eagleclaw picked up his blue-beaded, long-stemmed tobacco pipe which he lit with the glowing end of a stick from the fire. After he had sucked in enough to make the tobacco red, he passed it to Fast Otter who smoked and passed it to Rick, and then me, and on around the circle back to Eagleclaw. The burning tobacco hurt some of our throats, even some of the Indians, most boys coughing at least once. It was good, I thought suddenly, that I'd turned Dave onto pot. His throat was ready for strong Indian tobacco.

When the pipe came back to Eagleclaw, he sat down cross legged. We all imitated him as he held the pipe against his lap and said, "Our white brother Dave does not know our story, so we will tell it." Eagleclaw told the story he always told when a new guy sweated, a story he had put into his play, *Give Away*, about how the Great Spirit had given the people of Turtle Island the sweat lodge ceremony. He told it like a good storyteller, not talking too fast or too slow but in a soft and clear Indian rhythm. He told Dave about a woman in the First Times who became pregnant by eating a stone that was, actually, Grandfather Spirit; how she carried her child, Alosa, to term and how after he grew up a bit, she noticed he could talk with spirits in the rocks and boulders and the hard earth, so she called him "the stone boy." She also noticed he was always sad, missing his four uncles who had gone away to hunt and didn't return. One day, when he was "the age of you boys and men here today," Eagleclaw included all of us with both hands outstretched, Alosa missed his uncles so much he left his mother to search for them. Many weeks into this journey, he found his uncles in a round domed hut, guarded by Coyote woman.

Eagleclaw frowned ritualistically when he said Coyote woman. I saw that Dave was listening to the story intently, though still fidgeting.

"Coyote woman captured all of the uncles many years ago and wrapped them up paralyzed and unconscious in bundles of white shroud," Eagleclaw continued. "When Alosa saw that these were his lost uncles, he begged the cunning old woman to let them go free. Coyote woman said she would free them if Alosa took care of her like a slave. Alosa decided to do it, but one day, when she could tell he was becoming impatient with having to be her slave, she pulled out a knife to kill him. He was strong enough to defeat her. He shoved the knife into her chest. The old woman screamed but had no blood in her.

"Bloodless, heartless, her body became dead smoke and drifted away. As soon as he knew he was safe, Alosa yelled at the bundles and shook them, trying to wake them up. But the uncles didn't move. Now he worried he had killed the only person who could free them, so he prayed to Grandfather, and Grandfather heard him. 'I will help you,' Grandfather said, instructing Alosa to build a round hut that would be called a sweat lodge. 'You will find tree branches from the mountain roads. You will bend the branches. You will form a womb from the branches and cover it with buffalo blankets . . .'"

Interrupting his story, Eagleclaw said to Dave, "Our lodge here is covered with tarps and old quilts, but that is all right. Each piece is sanctified by the same Grandfather and Grandmother."

Dave nodded that he understood, his arms curled up against his body.

Eagleclaw continued, "Grandfather told the stone boy what steps to follow in a sweat ceremony—four rounds so that each of the four uncles could be revived. Alosa did the ceremony, and his uncles awoke, one in each round, then all five men went home, the uncles hugging their sister, Alosa, and telling her of the adventure. From that day onward, David McConnell, we Indians all around the country practice the sweat lodge ceremony as it will be practiced today. Grandfather, thank you for our traditions. We do not let our Indian traditions die, no matter how much alcohol we drink. We will protect our Indian heritage on Turtle Island."

I had been looking sideways at Dave while he listened to Eagleclaw's story, and it seemed to me that his eyes looked furtively at Eddie, the youngest boy at the sweat, a skinny thirteen-year-old wearing a black swimsuit. I couldn't be sure, but it seemed like Dave looked at Eddie in a way that seemed cold and warm at once, full of love and hate. And did Dave have an erection inside his swim trunks? As Dave's eyes moved away from Eddie, his hands moved in front of his bathing suit.

I had noticed Dave getting erections before—once while we got stoned in the basement, once when we had been talking about hurting Allen, and again in the Lester's barn that night. I knew what it was like to get erections at the weirdest times, but to get one here, now, with Eagleclaw telling this holy story . . .

*I hate you,* I hissed at Dave in my mind. *Why do we even hang out anymore?*

My stomach turned over with rage at myself for the thoughts. I felt almost like sobbing as Eagleclaw said, "For all our relations," his usual comment after a ritual, then all of us repeated back, "For all our relations."

Dave was late to respond, and his voice squeaked. Embarrassed, he apologized, avoided our eyes, shoving his hands together like a knife blade into his closed groin. No one said anything about his apology, which made Dave even more embarrassed.

"Today we enter the lodge with respect for all relations of all colors of skin and of heart," Eagleclaw continued. "Today, we will listen and speak with our brother spirits, all of them, Indian and Caucasian."

"Eagleclaw, you're a great storyteller, man," I said cheerfully.

"And you are a great listener, man," Eagleclaw quipped.

I laughed, and some boys joined in the release of tension.

Eagleclaw stood up, his knees popping, and all of us stood to join him.

I looked again at Dave who brushed at the front of his swim trunks like he was trying to push down on his groin.

Eagleclaw pulled his black bathing trunks off. Two of the other boys and I stripped naked, but the rest of the guys, including Dave, kept their bathing suits on.

Before my first sweat with Eagleclaw, I had asked if it was better to sweat naked or with clothes on. 'Many Indians are modest and do not show their private parts,' he had shrugged, 'and some prefer to be completely natural in the lodge. Neither way is better or worse.'

Like the other two naked boys, my hands vacillated between my hips and cupped together in front of my genitals. My penis was one of the only ones circumcised in all the sweat ceremonies I had done. At first this had bothered me, but it didn't now. I always pushed myself to be naked in locker rooms or at a sweat like this, just to show I didn't care about all that, or Dr. Francis.

Dave still had his black bathing shorts on but looked like he was sick with nervousness or pale with shame. Eagleclaw also noticed and asked if he was okay to proceed.

"I'm good," Dave said. "Yeah, I'm good."

Eagleclaw didn't seem sure, but accepted Dave's word.

"Dave McConnell, you are our brother in the lodge. If you become afraid in the dark, it is no shame. To leave the lodge like a warrior, you say, 'For all my relations,' and Fast Otter will let you out. So that no boy can be left outside the medicine circle today, if you leave the lodge, you sit outside and pray silently. Okay, Dave?"

Dave murmured thanks to Eagleclaw, his head bent down, his hands cupped in front of his shorts.

Eagleclaw's knees popped again as he got down on all fours and crawled into the lodge. He kissed the earth at the entrance, then crawled further in, putting himself right in front of the deep rock pit near the door. Then the rest of us got down and crawled into the crowded lodge.

Positioned between Dave and Bill, a sixteen-year-old, I could hear and feel everyone's breath and I could smell someone's BO and the smells of Eagleclaw's various herbs. Once Fast Otter brought in ten red-hot rocks with the pitchfork, he closed the door, and everything went dark. Within seconds we all sweated and breathed deeply, a little light coming off the red rocks but no other light anywhere, the place completely enclosed.

"Whoa! It's so hot!" Dave exclaimed in a trembling voice.

Eagleclaw chuckled, and Fast Otter said, "Not yet."

We heard a clink of Eagleclaw's hand bumping the bucket, and water splashed onto the hot rocks producing steam so hot our ears and faces felt like they were burning off.

Eagleclaw threw more water on the rocks.

Dave moaned, "Oh no!"

"Oh yes!" I laughed. "Oh yes, Grandfather, thank you!"

I felt like I got sometimes in the sweat lodge or when I smoked dope or read incredible books—feeling like flying into spiritual space and time, completely free with God floating with me, like someone who KNOWS everything, really knows! Eagleclaw threw more water on the rocks as I rocked back and forth happily, praying, "Oh God, please cure me. Oh God, this is it! This is so good. I will be so good."

"Grandfather," Eagleclaw intoned, "We have touched our rocks with sweet grass, sage, and ochsia in thanks for all the creatures—two-legged, four-legged, six-legged, eight-legged . . ." He went on and on, and I listened to his warm voice as if for the first time as he thanked Grandfather for all the insects, all the trees, all the flowers, the mountains, the sky, the earth, all the families of all the boys in this lodge, all the generations, the elders, the spirits, the sun and moon and stars and ancestors.

"Hey Grandfather!" he said when he was finished, and all of us murmured, "Hey Grandfather."

Eagleclaw asked, "Who will give thanks now?"

"Hey Grandfather!" Eddie whispered. "Thank you for helping me to be strong. Hey Grandfather!"

"Hey Grandfather," we all said in unison.

"Hey Grandfather," John said, his voice hoarse from the heat. "Thank you for ending the Vietnam war. Hey Grandfather!"

"Hey Grandfather!" I said. "Thank you for Eagleclaw's friendship and this lodge. Thank you for feeling so good. Hey Grandfather!"

After I finished, I realized I should have said something about Dave's friendship, but it was too late. All the other boys gave their thanks and then Eagleclaw threw more water onto the rocks. The lodge became so hot we didn't even know it as hot anymore—it had become something else, like arms wrapped around us.

"Hey Grandfather!" Dave said, choking. "Thanks for my mom . . . and everyone, including my dad and Eagleclaw. Hey Grandfather."

Eagleclaw let everything be silent for a second and then instructed Fast Otter to open the door flap.

Light blinded everyone while Fast Otter kissed the ground and said, "For all my relations," then crawled out the doorway.

As I crawled out of the lodge, my eyes adjusted, and I saw that all the boys were dripping with sweat. I kissed the ground, said, "For all my relations," then noticed that Dave didn't kiss the ground or say the line like he was supposed to. He just rushed toward the pond, dove in, and stayed under for a long time. I drank some water from the large plastic bottles we had filled up at the house, then went to him on the beach, laughing.

"Was that great or what, Dave!"

He grunted.

"What do you think of sweating, man?"

In my joy, I asked questions without waiting for answers, then talked with Fast Otter who sat nearby while we all rehydrated. Dave lay on the sand, the sun burning his zitty back. I felt the sun burning me too as Eagleclaw announced it was time for the "vision round."

Dave pushed up and moved quickly into the cool water again, making him the last guy besides Fast Otter to get back into the lodge.

From his place by the rocks, Eagleclaw smiled at Dave and said, "You are brave today."

Dave avoided everyone's eyes, faking a smile.

Fast Otter crawled into the lodge, brought the flap down so that the lodge again became completely dark except for a seam of light at the base of the door. Eagleclaw pointed it out to Fast Otter, who maneuvered the tarp door there by the rock pit, so the seam of light disappeared.

Now, in the pure dark, Eagleclaw threw more water on the new batch of red rocks, and we got incredibly hot again, sweat pouring down our bodies. Eagleclaw invited us to pray for vision. Fast Otter thanked the Otter spirit of the river for showing him the vision many weeks ago that he would leave the reservation and go to UCLA on a scholarship like Eagleclaw had gone to New York.

"Hey Grandfather!" Fast Otter finished.

"Hey Grandfather!" we all agreed.

"Hey Grandfather, I want to love people and the world," I said. "My vision is that I love people in the future. It's hard to do. Things get in the way. Grandfather, so many things get in the way. Things happen to me. I do bad things. Grandfather, I want to love people. I want to love everyone, really . . ." I thought I would say more, maybe even break the pact and reveal our secret, like some voice was telling me to do, but simply concluded with, "Hey Grandfather!"

"Hey Grandfather!" Dave followed. "Thank you for my science fiction stories. Hey Grandfather!"

Then Rick asked to be a good father to his child.

Then other voices asked for other visions or spoke visions they had.

Meanwhile, I noticed Dave fidgeting, and he cleared his throat very loudly. As Eddie started to talk about his vision, we all heard, "Help! Oh God, help."

"Dave?" Eagleclaw asked.

Dave yelled or whined, a panicky sound, "Oh no, please, stop."

"Fast Otter!" Eagleclaw barked. Fast Otter lifted the sweat lodge door, light pouring in.

Dave clawed at the air, trying to get outside, his arms like flags flailing in the wind and his body shaking.

We rushed to him on the sand while he tried to speak in a boy's squeaking voice, "Huhhhhuhh," and fell next to the pond floundering, his tongue out as if he were panting for water.

"David!" Eagleclaw yelled, running to him.

Dave's eyes suddenly closed, and he became still on the sand.

"What's happening, Eagleclaw?" I yelled, my hands touching Dave's forehead like they had that night when he yelled about Allen.

Eagleclaw bent and slapped Dave's face gently. Dave's mouth foamed, and he convulsed at least a dozen times, then lay motionless.

"David!" Eagleclaw yelled.

John came over with a water jug, and Eagleclaw emptied it on Dave's face.

"Dave!" I moaned.

John rushed to the pond to get more water.

For a panicked moment, I was sure Dave had died.

# CHAPTER 11

"IS DAVE OKAY?" Harvey asked two hours later. He saw how shocked I still felt after driving Dave to the hospital in Durango. "Are *you* okay?" he asked, holding me tight until I broke the hug.

"I'm okay. Dave's okay."

"Talk to me. What happened?"

"It was so weird! I thought he died, but the doctor said he just got really dehydrated."

I wolfed down a sandwich, drank milk and OJ, and reported everything about the lodge—how Dave got sick and Eagleclaw held him and gave him water, and how on the way to the hospital Dave had moaned in my car, talking to himself about the same priest his mother had mentioned to me earlier in the summer, Father Kordash, who had taught Dave how to play the piano.

"What about Father Kordash?" Harvey probed.

"Dave didn't make sense, but he was sad, I know that. He moaned, 'Don't leave! Why did you leave?'" Harvey asked more questions as we munched on chips and peanuts until there wasn't anything else to talk about.

"What a day you've had," he concluded, giving me another hug.

He saw that I wanted to get away, go down to my basement haven, so he returned to his scripts and accounting spreadsheets on the kitchen table and let me clomp downstairs to the basement.

---

I listened to the Beatles' *Abbey Road* but didn't really hear any of the songs, just sat there thinking about the floating feeling I had in the sweat lodge. Right there, in the middle of that beautiful feeling, Grandfather's voice had told me I had to tell my secret. It wasn't like I really heard a voice, I knew that, but it was an insight, a clear thought: *God wants you to tell your secret.*

I sat in my basement listening to music and trying to understand how this could be true. And if it were true, who should I tell? Obviously, I couldn't tell another kid—telling Dave had only made things worse. And I couldn't tell Judith. The truth would hurt her too much, both truths—that I was a weird kid who got involved in a bad thing with Allen Tremmel, and that it was her who made me go see "my abuser," Dr. Francis. And what if she decided I was weird for doing what I did with Dr. Francis, too? What if she wondered why I didn't get out of there, why I didn't tell her what we were doing? What if she thought I liked it? And what if she hated me for what I did to Allen? She would hate me for sure—I had become the violent man she hated.

No, I couldn't tell her.

Could I tell Harvey about Dr. Francis? Harvey sat upstairs always wanting to be "a good dad," my friend. Could I tell him everything? Would he hate me? *You are messed up*, the voice said inside me. *You are so messed up! Tell Harvey. He'll help you.* But no, no, I couldn't tell anyone. No. Dave and I had a pact. Besides, anyone I told would hate me. They would think I was sick to do stuff with Dr. Francis and even more sick to do stuff to Allen.

I decided to go upstairs to test myself, my nauseous stomach like a huge fist pushing around inside me. I found Harvey outside on the two-person swinging chair reading the play *Rhinoceros* by Ionesco in a slim blue and white paperback book.

"How are you doing?" he asked, looking at me over the top of his half-moon reading glasses and patting the chair next to him.

"Okay," I said.

"You didn't get stoned," he said, looking at my eyes and seeing no redness.

"Can I ask you something?" I said, moving to the chair.

"Of course."

He took his glasses off, shoved them down into the V at the top of his vest.

"Do you think a kid or an adult can actually feel 'good' or 'evil' inside him when he's, like, in church or in a temple or maybe in a sweat lodge?" Using my fingers like tiny prongs I made quotation marks in the air for 'good' and 'evil.'

Harvey cocked his head to the right, trying to figure out what I meant. "Like actually feel good or evil inside your soul?" he asked, touching his chest at the heart.

"Yeah. I mean, in the sweat lodge, before Dave went ballistic, I had a feeling, like maybe it was light exploding, which sounds lame, but something like that. Like I floated, and everything felt great, like the absolute good, like I could hear God talking to me. It was a feeling of not being bad or evil or a screw up, you know?"

"You've thought you were evil or a screw up?"

"No! Jesus, I'm just saying, it was a feeling like where it's not possible I could be bad or evil, ever. Like I was . . . I don't know, man, I can't describe it. Maybe I just made it up in my head because I want to be different from Dave who is weird, you know, such a misfit?"

Harvey tried to follow my thoughts, encouraging me as he bit the inside of his lip. "If you mean you felt a spiritual feeling, where you feel completely alive, completely . . . 'at one with the universe,' yeah, I get that feeling in the sweat lodge. Is that what you mean?"

"I guess so, yeah. It's like, the Self."

He nodded. "It's interesting that you associate it with good and evil, Ben. I never thought of it that way. I just thought of it as a kind of dreamy, spiritual feeling I get sometimes. But you think of it as good versus evil, or something like that?"

"Yeah, I guess."

"How come you think that? Do you think about good and evil a lot?"

*Wasn't I supposed to?* It seemed like Harvey didn't think this made sense. "Not a lot," I covered. "Just sometimes."

"Tell me more. You associate evil with being a screw up? I sure felt like a screw up at your age."

"Really?" He had mentioned before that he drifted around from theater group to theater group and never quite made it. Was this what he meant? He hadn't talked before about feeling like a screw up as a kid. He didn't talk much about his childhood with me.

"Oh yeah, don't get me started on my screw ups," he said, a refrain he often repeated. "But tell me what you're thinking. It seems like you're understanding about evil in the world. Is this what you're doing? You're seventeen. It's the right time to figure out what evil is."

Now we got closer to what happened with Allen, and I could have said something to him right then, right there, but my stomach turned over.

*I couldn't. I just couldn't.*

"I gotta figure it out for sure," I said, standing up and ending the conversation abruptly. "Thanks, man. I'm gonna get something to drink. You want a Coke?"

"No thanks. Wait, though. You sure you don't wanna talk more?"

I leaned over and gave him a hug, which always satisfied him. "Later, maybe."

I went inside, got a Coke from the fridge, and walked downstairs to the basement. I thought about putting music on again but instead opened up *Siddhartha,* reading pages from various chapters before I settled on Chapter Seven, where Siddhartha was not a kid anymore, and Vasudeva, the old ferry man at the river, had a deep talk with him about Om, the sound of God.

Oh yeah, here it was, the feeling I was trying to describe. *When Siddhartha listened attentively to the river, to its song of a thousand voices, the great song of a thousand voices consisted of one word: Om—perfection.* I closed my eyes and tried to recreate the beautiful feeling I had gotten in the sweat lodge. It was the same feeling I had when Dave and I drove up into the mountains that seemed so beautiful and blue to us early in the summer and felt the wind on our faces and were so happy.

*Is that God?*

I read more and saw Siddhartha who confessed everything about his life to Vesudeva by the river. He talked and talked with the old man, then felt much better as Vasudeva listened carefully. Vasudeva didn't judge, he just listened. He wasn't a mother or father, both of whom would have a million emotions if they listened. He was someone else, someone like a priest or rabbi, a spiritual man. He had brown skin, and he was old, and—

Oh.

Was it meant to be?

The voice in the lodge told me I had to tell someone other than Dave, I just had to. I couldn't be good and true and have a Self unless I acted like Alosa and killed the Coyote woman and became a good man who started over. Yes, that is what I had to do, and this is why God told me to open up the Hermann Hesse book and read the last chapter of it, yes, yes.

Eagleclaw.

I could tell him everything—or almost everything, some things just couldn't be told—and I could swear him to secrecy right there at the pond.

Yes.

I closed my eyes and pictured him sitting wrinkled and brown on the old sagging chair, his black eyes and thick glasses as close to Vesudeva as I would get in my life. Harvey didn't understand what I was getting at, and I didn't want to hurt my mother by telling her, but Eagleclaw—I could tell him.

But what about the pact?

Oh man, the pact.

# CHAPTER 12

THE NEXT DAY Harvey and I went to the gym for rehearsal. Jimmie Wild Elk had not drunk too much that morning, and my father seemed relieved. I prompted Jimmie from the prompter's script when he forgot a line. Jimmie did a good job with Albee's *American Dream* monologue, but his voice faded. "Remember, Jimmie," my father directed. "Your voice will stand against all the colonialist hoopla of the bicentennial year, so you are more than one actor. You stand for the whole Indian nation. Give it that passion, please."

During the lunch break, Harvey gave me the keys to the Dart. I drove to Eagleclaw's house, my stomach turning over every five minutes. Above the desert, the sun shined like a white gauzy ball behind thin clouds. The sagebrush and mesas and reddish dirt lay covered with the dull shine from the sky. The temperature was over ninety, heat rising off the pavement. There was one antelope out by a cactus and some vultures, otherwise very few animals or vehicles moving on the Rez.

Hot wind hit my face, and I murmured pieces of the Albee play, then whispered lines from the Tao Te Ching. *The Tao marches without moving, it rolls up its sleeve without showing the arm, captures the enemy without attacking, the Tao is an army without weapons.* The words helped me be less afraid of telling Eagleclaw everything, though I kept thinking I would vomit any minute.

When I arrived at Eagleclaw's place, he spotted me and came to his front screen door. "Ben," he smiled, shaking hands as he always did, wearing his ragged black shorts with no shirt. He pushed his glasses up his sweaty nose as I followed him through his living room where wood and old appliances sat around to be repaired, dust coating everything. "I am glad you came today, my friend. How is Dave?"

"He's in the hospital, but he's okay. He got really dehydrated, like you thought. At least that's what the doctors said. I'm gonna go back and see him later today."

"Dave is not healthy," Eagleclaw nodded. "He must sleep and eat more, and he must drink more water."

"His parents are with him now."

"Thank you for letting me know about his health," Eagleclaw said.

As we sat and drank coffee, I gazed around his place. There were different kinds of drums leaning against a wall and photos of Eagleclaw in an Army uniform, one of his ex-wife, and one of his son in war paint. On another wall was his gun rack with rifles hung at about six feet up. Underneath it sat the dresser that stored his boxes of bullets we had stolen from.

"You are thinking many thoughts, Ben," Eagleclaw said, his eyes magnified by the glasses as usual. "Are you worried about Dave?"

"I guess," I nodded, silent for a few seconds while he waited.

*Could I really tell him some of my bad stuff?*

I stared at the gun rack, took a sip of coffee, and said, "Eagleclaw, you remember last week when Dave and I were here?" I tested the words, pausing after them, waiting to see if my stomach would get worse or better.

"Which time?" he asked.

I felt no change in myself and continued, "The time you and I talked a little bit, and I said some stuff about 'water in a cage' like a dork, and you said, 'Today is not the day for truth.' You remember?"

"I remember."

Eagleclaw lowered his coffee cup, holding it on his lap with both hands.

Out the window beside the gun rack, I noticed a fish splash in the pond.

Eagleclaw waited for me to continue.

Finally, looking into his eyes again, I said softly, "The point is, man, I need help."

He nodded, waiting.

"The thing is, I did . . . I mean, *we*, Dave and me, we did something that's really . . . really, messing with my head, you know? I think it's like confession, I think I've got to tell someone. In the sweat lodge, I felt so good, and it was like I heard a voice, you know? Like Grandfather. I mean, you know, not really a voice, but—"

"What did you do, Ben?"

"Oh man," I moaned, taking in a deep breath, mustering the words I had rehearsed on the drive out here. "The point is, well, when I got here to Durango, I was scared and lonely, you know, like I always am when I come to Harvey's towns. I feel stupid now, but I needed a friend, and Dave was supposed to be this 'meant to be' friend. He was brilliant, kind of dorky looking for sure, but so smart, smarter than me in a lot of ways. You know?"

I described Dave the first day I met him at his fort that looked like a sweat lodge, how we got to be friends who did everything together, even how we got stoned a lot and talked. I told Eagleclaw how Dave talked in his sleep about Allen Tremmel, and how Dave had the guts to tell me everything about him. "I think this Tremmel guy is evil," I said. "I hope so. God, I hope so."

Eagleclaw drank his coffee and continued to listen patiently.

"I wanted to help Dave," I pushed forward. "Like, I wanted to protect my little brother, help make the world right. I wanted to teach the bully a lesson. I had lots of motivations, you know, competing motivations, but what Allen did to Dave, it was so bad, man," and I described the razors in the locker room and the lagoon.

Eagleclaw's face became pale, but he just said, "Go on, Ben."

I told him how Dave and I wrote a script and devised a plan. Then I told him how our script called for us to do a bad thing to Allen, and that at the time it didn't seem too bad to just hit a guy who had done the same to Dave.

Then, coughing, almost crying, my stomach nauseous, I described the extra things Dave made Allen do and how they scared me.

Dropping my face down, I said, "Dave even started putting the gun inside Allen's . . . Man, it was way too weird. It's like Dave wanted to do like Allen did to him, with the fishing pole. It's logical, I guess, but it weirded me out."

For a few seconds I stopped talking and debated whether I should keep going or run away. I hadn't said anything about stealing the bullets from Eagleclaw, nor had I mentioned Dr. Francis.

I could run.

Eagleclaw set his cup onto the table, folded his hands on his lap, and asked me to continue.

My coffee cup was empty by now, and I clasped it in my hands as I leaned forward, my elbows anchored against each of my knees. I hadn't realized it, but I had gone into nearly a sitting fetal position on the couch. In my long silence, Eagleclaw took off his glasses, rubbing his eyes with his right thumb and forefinger.

"This is bad, Ben. I understand. But there is more. Tell me, please. It is better to tell someone."

I set my coffee cup down on the floor, crossed my legs lotus style under me on the couch, and stared down at the chipped wooden floor.

"I'm not gay," I said. "So, this thing I'm about to tell you, it's got to be why I even agreed to help Dave in the first place, right? Because of what happened to me when I was a kid?"

Eagleclaw's face showed a lack of comprehension.

"What I'm about to tell you—it's got to be why the extra stuff Dave wanted to do to Allen really weirded me out, see, because Dr. Francis, I gotta tell you about Dr. Francis, man. I mean, I thought telling Dave would help, but it made things worse, so, why am I telling you? I don't know. God, I don't know. I just have to tell you. I just want to feel good some time in my life, you know?"

"Yes, Ben. Please tell me. I will help you."

A few minutes passed, and I heard, "and he touched my privates," and I realized I was talking, and my eyes were watering as I described my relationship with Dr. Francis all the way to the touching and masturbating but not farther—I just could NOT tell anyone about the blow jobs—and luckily I didn't have to because I had started to cry right then.

Eagleclaw stood up, brought me a towel, and sat next to me on the couch. "Ben, it is good to cry. It is okay, son." If he had brought my chest to his chest and cooed at me right then, I would have died from shame, but Eagleclaw just sat with me as I wiped drool off my beard.

"Am I evil, Eagleclaw?" I asked, clutching the towel in my fists. "Your son, Clayton, he wouldn't have done what Dave and I did, right? Am I messed up? Like, did Dr. Francis mess me up? I mean, in the sweat lodge, I have beautiful feelings, and I get that feeling sometimes like when I read *Siddhartha* or listen to music or write in my journal or get stoned, like everything is good and real and cool, but I'm . . . I don't know . . . why would I even do something bad to Allen if Dr. Francis hadn't, like, made me evil or something?"

Eagleclaw shook his head, agreeing but disagreeing.

"You hurt another boy's soul, Ben, but you are not evil. If you were evil, you would not talk about these things and you would not feel bad about what you did. Ben, you feel these feelings because you have a conscience."

That sounded right, but I insisted, "What if I can't stop myself from doing evil things in my life later on? Like look at Dave—I didn't stop Dave from doing what he did to Allen. I mean, look at *me*—I went along with the plan all the way."

Eagleclaw shook his head. "You are not evil, but you have just now told me many things. There is much to pray about." He went silent, thinking, which worried me.

"I'm sorry," I said. "I have too much bad stuff in my head. I shouldn't have told you."

Eagleclaw stood up suddenly, took his pack of cigarettes off the little kitchen table, and walked out his back door. Confused by his leaving, I rushed out to catch up and follow him down his footpath towards the sweat lodge and pond. "Where are you going?" I cried in panic as he walked to his little chairs at the edge of the pond.

"Sit here," he ordered, pointing me to the chair beside him, sitting down, lighting a cigarette and looking out at the pond. I dropped into the other chair, avoiding looking at him or the pond or at anything except my knees, feet and sandals.

"When did you decide to capture Allen Tremmel?" he asked.

I sucked in phlegm through my nostrils and said, "About a month ago, the second week of July. Dave told me about what Allen did to him, and we started thinking about what to do to Allen. I went down to the furniture store and scoped him out. It's like the thing just started happening in our heads. I told Dave about Dr. Francis three weeks ago, and that made me want to help Dave all the way. That's kind of how it all happened."

Eagleclaw blew smoke out, nodding his head. "You did wrong, Ben. You know this. But the doctor also did wrong. Allen and his friends did wrong. Dave did wrong. You thought you could become like a stone boy, a spiritual boy, through your actions. I understand that."

"Yes, yes, I think I tried to be a sacred warrior. I tried to be like the stone boy in the story, on a sacred mission. I mean, isn't that what I was trying to do? Or like the Tao? I mean, sometimes I felt like I wanted to be a warrior, like a path of the heart in Carlos Castenada, or in your play, *Give Away*, you know, like your son was brave . . ."

Eagleclaw's voice interrupted, sharp, loud. "Ben, stop talking about all these other things. Right now, you will stop!"

"Yes, yes, sorry."

Eagleclaw tended to be quiet, free of any emotions except always some kind of grief, but now he was angry, so I must have missed what he was trying to tell me. I stopped and waited as he sucked on the cigarette so that it glowed red.

"You will have to speak with your father about what you've done," he said finally. "And you will have to tell him about what happened when you were a little boy with Dr. Francis."

"No way! I can't tell Harvey. I just told *you*, that's enough. I promise I won't talk about Carlos Castaneda anymore. I'm sorry. Please don't be mad at me."

Eagleclaw frowned, concentrating. "Ben, I am not angry at you. I am angry at Dr. Francis and Allen Tremmel. I am glad you came to me, Ben, but it is wrong for me to talk to you about this without your father . . ." At the word father, his thoughts suddenly seemed to drift. "We had a priest on our reservation, a man, a 'Father,' named Jerry Brown. He harmed some boys . . ."

Eagleclaw stopped himself, thinking about something he didn't reveal, then he returned to his former track. "I am not your father. Harvey Brickman is your father. This is what I am saying. You must speak to your *real* father."

"No way," I said reflexively.

"You will now talk with your father," Eagleclaw said, turning his head to me. "My son and I . . . things would be different now if we had talked of these bad things when he was a boy. I know of these bad things."

*What did he mean?*

Eagleclaw paused again and then said, "Evil is a very important part of this, but there is more, and these things you and your father must decide. You are not evil, Ben, but David and Allen Tremmel and Dr. Francis . . . they have control of you. You are going down a bad road. You know this."

He turned to me, looked at me again with those huge spectacled eyes. "This is why you came to me. You trust me, so I will act in the most trustworthy way. I will not tell anyone about this, but I will tell your father. Even if you decide never to come to my land again, Ben, I will not do the wrong thing for you like I did with my son. I will not!"

His voice was so vehement as he turned back away from me towards the pond. In that moment, I realized that I didn't really know him, not at all. What was he really talking about? He'd lived with us back in New York long ago, and I'd read his play and hung out with him and sweated with him, but I didn't know him or his son.

*What had happened to his son?*

"I guess I should leave," I offered, standing up. "I'll tell my dad. I'll go tell him right now."

Eagleclaw stood up too, sensing I was lying.

"I will go with you. I will get a shirt and my sandals, and we will go to the gym."

Eagleclaw abruptly walked toward the house, and I followed him thinking that I could just run faster than him and jump in the car and get away.

"Dr. Francis is very bad," Eagleclaw said as I trailed behind him. "He has done many more things than you describe, I am sure of this. He will 'mess with the heads of many boys,' as you call it. This is very bad."

Suddenly, he stopped, turned, grasped my arm.

"Ben, you must be a man and do something about this Dr. Francis. This is part of your duty now. You must tell the police in New York what happened to you."

"I'll be a man," I promised, simultaneously regretting that I'd come here and talked.

Eagleclaw grunted and walked into the house as I froze thinking there was no way out now unless I killed Eagleclaw and buried his body out here—

*Jesus!*

The thought sickened me, and I pushed it back. I would have to tell Harvey, but I needed to make sure neither he nor Eagleclaw told my mother because . . .

"Let us go to the gym now," Eagleclaw said, dressed in his black shirt and brown sandals. "I am sorry you were confused so much by the doctor. He tried to take away your soul and put it into his own body. I am very sorry about this. I could not help another, but I can help you. It is very important to me that you came to me. Thank you, Ben."

"You bet," I nodded automatically, looking downward as I walked with him to my car. In the dirt below me, an ant carried a white morsel. Another one moved behind it, zig-zagging as we got to the car.

We drove away as Eagleclaw said, "I know you better now that you have done this telling today. You have courage, Ben. You tried to learn your own soul by smoking marijuana and reading books and watching television and playing games and doing sweats with me and thinking inside your own mind about spiritual things. But now you are a boy who has done something bad. This bad thing will make you learn your soul better than thinking and sweating and marijuana."

"Sure, you're right," I said reflexively. "That makes sense." My stomach was nauseous again, almost like I would puke.

"You and your father will decide how to talk to Dave and his family. If you do not talk to Dave, I can talk to Dave after you go to New York. Dave will come to see me. I am sure of this."

"I don't think so, man."

"He will."

"How do you know?"

"Because he has left here something he will return for."

"What did he leave?"

"Dave has left his dignity here. He will want it returned to him."

I wasn't even sure if *I* would ever come back here so Dave definitely would not come. He wouldn't want to see the Indians again. Eagleclaw was weirding out about something regarding his own son and he was wrong about Dave.

And he was not Vasudeva.

But why did I suddenly have an urge to hug Eagleclaw's skinny brown body?

I couldn't stop myself.

I stopped the car in the middle of the dirt road, put it in park, and reached over to hug him.

He hugged me back and he didn't let go, just held me, murmuring, "I am sorry, my son. I am so sorry. But your father can help you. My son, your father can help you. You are not evil, Ben. It is going to be okay. It will be okay . . ."

# CHAPTER 13

DRIVING BACK TO THE GYM with Eagleclaw, I rehearsed in my head what to tell Harvey. When we got close to the gym, I couldn't find any plan that protected everybody, and I felt exhausted from trying to figure everything out. Eagleclaw sat silently, smoking his Marlboros, and I said I felt bad about betraying Dave. Eagleclaw said Dave would understand, at some point, that I was doing the right thing. But couldn't Eagleclaw see? No matter what I did now that I had told Eagleclaw, someone would be betrayed.

"Dammit!" I slammed the brakes. A teenage bike rider pulled out of the gym parking lot right in front of me as I pulled in. Eagleclaw slammed his feet into the floor as if he could press the brakes too. The bike rider didn't seem to notice, just riding away as we parked, got out of the car, and walked to the gym door.

"God, I hope this is the right thing," I murmured to Eagleclaw, but he focused on the gym door, not my misgivings or whining. I stood behind him, letting him approach Harvey first, as he said he would do, my stomach nauseous and my arm pits stinking with sweat. While Eagleclaw talked to Harvey, I walked back outside, waiting, knowing Eagleclaw would get his way, and soon Harvey would come out and find me.

Five minutes later, he did. Harvey and Eagleclaw walked out into the dirt and dead grass where I waited for them. Harvey wore black jeans, his brown leather vest, and his turquoise bolo tie. His hair was tied back in his ponytail with a rubber band, more strands of gray running through it than a couple months ago.

"Ben, what's wrong? Eagleclaw says you need to talk to me."

His voice was impatient—he had things to do—but he looked like he was a little worried too.

"It's weird stuff, Harvey," I said as Eagleclaw stood next to him, waiting.

I thought about not saying anything at all, stonewalling somehow, but I shifted on my feet, kneaded my hands in front of me, and just started talking about becoming friends with Dave, him talking in his sleep, his confession of what Allen did to him. I kept my head lowered as I told, but I could see Harvey's eyes widen as he listened silently. I was scared and I had been scared all the way from Eagleclaw's to the gym, but now I felt relieved. Talking to Eagleclaw and now my father, I didn't feel as bad as I thought I would.

When I got to telling Harvey about what Dave and I did to Allen, he couldn't listen quietly anymore.

"Why would *you* get involved like that? Jesus, Ben! You made him . . . strip naked!"

"There is more to understand," Eagleclaw said calmly to Harvey, touching his arm.

I turned away from my father's eyes, looked out at the desert—the sand, the low cacti, the dirty brown sagebrush, the shacks and poverty and Indians walking slowly. In a voice that seemed far away from me, I tried to explain to my father how I thought my "motivation" came from "what happened with Dr. Francis."

I explained how I didn't like doing the things Dr. Francis wanted, but that he told me he would send me to a mental asylum.

Harvey's face went from shocked to angry to worried to sad and then to all of them at once. When he heard my lie about me getting out of Dr. Francis' office before giving the blow jobs, he held his head with both hands.

"My God, Ben. Oh no. You must have been so scared."

Eagleclaw saw that Harvey would let me tell the story, so he went to the gym to give us privacy and to tell the people who had come out of the gym that rehearsal was over.

"We've got to get out of here," Harvey realized as two actors approached him.

I got in the car, shivering and shaking as Harvey went back to the gym to retrieve his briefcase. Eagleclaw came over to my side of the car. "You are a brave boy, Ben. Remember, you are not evil."

"Thanks," I said, wishing he would leave now, wishing I had never told him anything, but grateful too. Harvey came back with his briefcase and thanked Eagleclaw who nodded his head silently and went back to the gym to find a ride home.

Harvey drove us away from the reservation, back toward the pine trees of Durango. He asked lots of questions, wanting to know everything. "How much did this Dr. Francis touch you, Ben? How many times? You've got to tell me. You've got to trust me, Ben. Did he do more with you? Have you told me everything?"

I deflected him with, "It wasn't much," and watched trees pass by like quick shadows. "You can't tell Mom, though," I said. "It will kill her. Promise me you won't tell her."

"You're very protective of your mother."

I bored my eyes into the side of his face. "You've got to promise you won't tell her!"

"Okay. Okay, Ben."

"No! Promise me, please!"

He relented. "Against my better judgment, I'll promise."

"I gotta trust you, Dad." I looked over at my father with the silver goatee and graying hair and watery eyes, this man I used to call "Daddy."

"Ben, I promise."

He looked me in the eye and then had to turn back to the road.

"The point is, the doctor touched me maybe five times," I lied, "then he played with me when I had a boner a few times, then he had me beat him off. It was just for a month or so, once a week. That was it. Luckily, right?"

"Nothing else? Just touching and mutual masturbation?"

"Yeah."

"Are you sure?"

"I'd know," I frowned. "Okay!"

He slammed his right palm on the steering wheel. "Jesus!"

"I hated it," I said, "but it felt good too. That was so weird."

*Why had I admitted that?*

"Of course it felt good," he said, not surprised. "He taught you how to masturbate, and masturbation feels good. You and I talked about that years ago. But I didn't know about this, Ben. Jesus! We've got to tell the police. That doctor could be doing even worse things to other kids."

"But then Mom would know!"

"Oh Ben, I'm so sorry," he moaned. "It's my fault. I was in Vancouver. We'd just gotten divorced." He was remembering, not paying attention to me. "If I'd taken you with me . . . dammit. I told your mother I should take you with me that year! You were a boy, I'm your father. Dammit!"

"It's okay," I soothed.

Harvey was driving eighty now, the old Dart shuddering.

"Slow down, man."

He took his foot off the accelerator, the car slowing immediately.

"And it's not like I'm totally mental, you know," I pointed out stupidly. "I mean, I can be cool with this stuff as long as no one else knows. And anyway, I'm not, you know, gay. I only like girls."

"You're not gay, I know that," Harvey agreed, "but that's not the issue. I've spent my life among gay people, and I love them.

Truthfully, I'm more worried you'd become homophobic than gay. Ben," he turned to me, "You have been with a girl, right?"

"Jesus, Dad."

"Well, have you?"

"Stop!"

"I'm just trying to understand. What if it *can* change you— inside? I mean, look how violent you boys were with Allen. Ben, I don't know much about this kind of thing, what the . . . psychological ramifications are. You have to see someone, get some help. Even if you bypass telling your mother for now, you have to talk to some other professional."

"Like another psychiatrist! Are you crazy?"

"Not necessarily a psychiatrist."

"No way!"

"God, okay, I know. You're right. But we've got to think about a counselor. I saw a counselor after your mom and I broke up. I felt . . . I felt guilty about some things. I felt so . . . ashamed. I mean, I was culpable in the break up. I had to figure things out. A counselor really helped."

"I'm not seeing a counselor, Harvey," I said it emphatically.

*But what things did he feel guilty about?* Judith told me she was mad at him for sleeping with someone in one of the troupes. When I confronted him about it one summer, he told me he did this after he and Judith had separated.

"Then what do we do?" my father exhaled loudly. "We can't just do nothing, not tell anyone else, go on with our lives as they were."

"Yes, we can. We have to."

"I could call my friend Dawson Fitts, at Stanford," he kept going as if I hadn't said anything. "I could ask him questions without telling the whole story. He's a psychiatrist. I could talk to him, but you wouldn't have to."

"You gotta stop over-thinking this," I hissed. "I'm okay. I don't want you to tell anyone else. Dr. Francis is done with. We don't have to do anything else about that. The issue is what we do about Dave and Allen. That's the issue."

"Jesus, Ben. You kids could go to jail for what you did to Allen!"

Hearing him say the truth, then avoiding his eyes, my brain clicked on how bad and weird we were, and my eyes began to fill with water. *Dammit!* I put my hands over my face, hoping to stop them but couldn't. "Oh God," I murmured, my chin quivering. Harvey reached over to touch my shoulder, but I shrugged him off.

"Ben, it's going to be okay," Harvey said, pulling the car to the shoulder and shoving it into park. He put his arms around me and then the crying came fast, and I felt my daddy rocking me like I was a baby. I was so glad he rocked me, I grabbed his vest with my fingers, crying against his chest and chin.

"Oh Ben," he whispered in a choking voice, "Oh Ben, I'm such a screw up. Oh Ben, I'm so sorry."

We both cried until I finally sucked in my tears, getting them to stop. He let me go, scooting back over to his seat and wiping his eyes with the back of his hand. Thankfully, the tears seemed to be finished. Outside my window I saw a herd of antelope grazing, about ten of them.

"Ben, I've done bad things myself. We all have. We have to work through this, so it doesn't haunt you the rest of your life."

I sucked in my phlegm, turning back to him. "You did bad things?"

"Oh yes," he sighed. "So many." He didn't say anymore, just thinking.

"But you didn't do anything like I did," I said, probing at him as he stared straight ahead, hands clutching the steering wheel.

"What is the right thing to say right now? I don't know, Ben."
He turned to me, looking into my eyes.

"I don't know what a father is supposed to do right now. I don't know what a teenager is supposed to do. I wonder if you should rebel against your mother and me more? Would that help? Would that make it so that you don't have to get carried along in things and with people the way you do?"

"Carried along?"

Not till I heard myself ask the question did I understand what he meant.

"You do what other people want too much, I think. But Ben, I don't want you thinking about how you messed things up. You did nothing to make Dr. Francis do what he did. You know? That was not your fault, and you mustn't spend your life ashamed of it."

"Yeah, I know," I said reflexively, but if I hadn't made my parents get divorced, Mom never would have had to take me to Dr. Francis. Wasn't that the psychology of it? Mom told me a hundred times that kids think they are the cause of their parents' divorces, but they never were. 'It's us adults, Benny, not you kids,' she'd said. 'Never think you caused us to break up. This was not your fault.' But I always thought it.

Harvey let his breath out in a deep sigh.

"Ben, the bad things are bad, but they're not what it's all about. When I was young like you, I escaped my mistakes and I escaped my mother—your grandmother—by becoming an exhibitionist and pretending I was being completely open with the world. But I never told people who I really was, and my father, an accountant, couldn't understand my rebellions. And your mom married me for my rebelliousness, my independence, my dreams, but in the end, she hated my rebellions. Only when she understood I had to find myself did she let me be, and even 'finding yourself' is a big lie, too. You get to a point where you realize you are living lots of lies and they always haunt you."

What exactly was he talking about?

Rebellions?

Lies?

In the past, about his boyhood, he had told me normal stuff, like how he played baseball on the streets in Brooklyn, how his parents yelled at each other a lot, how his friends Harry and Grayson got him into the theater. I breathed quietly as he continued.

"I actually think you're a better person than I was at your age," Harvey said as he turned to me again for a second. "If I had been in your situation at seventeen, I probably would have wanted to teach a bully a lesson but would have been too scared to do it. I was undeveloped and small at that age. I was skinny and weak like Dave. In my generation, we had Errol Flynn and John Wayne, but guys like me wanted to be rebels like Marlon Brando or James Dean. But we could never live up to those guys. With you," he glanced at me, "I don't know . . . you guys have the freedom we fought for on the streets, and you're more mature, but you and your generation, you're not free."

I didn't understand this last part but didn't pursue it, wanting him to feel better.

"You wouldn't have gone psycho like Dave and I did."

"I don't know," Harvey said. "It doesn't sound like you went psycho. It sounds like you are still way better put together than Dave. Dave went psycho.

"One thing I've learned from my life," Harvey said, pushing his hair back with both hands, "these books and plays we devote our lives to, this art, these words on a page—they're real. Human beings are capable of any evil and any good. Pinter, Eunesco, Albee . . . they're writing plays that stand universally against the people who don't realize there's a lot of complexity to life, lots more than

Richard Nixon wants to admit. Sexual love is not immoral, but in the hands of Dr. Francis, it can be. Good and evil are often gray, not just black and white, or us versus them, but some things are just wrong . . ."

He kept talking and I tried to follow him because talking like this took him out of his sadness, and I didn't want him to feel like everything was his fault, and besides, he hadn't talked with me like this in years. Before the divorce, he used to stand up and act like Hamlet or Lear and give big speeches to me about why we were marching against the war and why we fought for women's liberation, but since the divorce he always seemed a little sad and I missed his speeches.

". . . Vietnam taught us we need to fight against the people who try to control us with their own fears, people who think life can't be 'groked' like you boys like to say, and you know what? Life is a mystery. There are no simple answers. People like Ionesco and Shakespeare and Albee try to elevate life in their art, they don't want a worldview to be forced on us, they want freedom, and freedom means everyone has to make mistakes."

He turned to me, finally getting to his point. "You have to make your mistakes, Ben, and you've made some, and we all do. It's painful, but life has to be lived. You are trying to live your life, despite the trauma your selfish parents put you through—"

"You aren't selfish," I interrupted. "No way."

"Yes I am. Don't kid yourself. I'm work obsessed. I have my demons. I've made bad mistakes. When I was your age, I had a good friend, Tony Beilerson, a real sensitive kid like I was. But one thing we didn't know anything about was protecting each other—"

Harvey looked out the windshield at his memories like he saw them perfectly in the glass. "I could never help Tony when he needed me. I just watched while he got his pants pulled down and kicked by a bully. Afterwards, Tony ran away across the grass, trying to get his pants up. I was small and couldn't fight against four big guys, so I just watched everything. I hated myself for a lot of years because of my weakness."

He paused, breathing in. A truck whooshed past us, shaking the car.

"A boy's world is tough, Ben," he continued. "I'm proud you're not a kid who gets picked on. I hate what you did to Allen, but I feel in my heart . . ." he hit his chest with his fist, almost breaking his glasses hanging there, "it shows there's something strong in you that's going to make you a survivor, a guy who thrives."

He paused, looking at me again.

"I guess that's all I have to say. I don't know if I'm helping you. And it still doesn't solve our problem—do we tell anyone about Allen?"

"So, you don't think Dave and I were evil with Allen?"

"You're not evil," he said. "I can't believe Dave is evil either, but there's something going on with him, depression maybe. Or . . . something. But you're not evil, Ben. You're growing up while you're awake, not asleep. That's crucial. You did wrong things with Allen, but you were hurt, you were angry, and you stumbled into it. It's not part of your character. You're a good kid, Ben."

Hearing those words from him, I trusted my father's opinion. All my worries about telling him about Allen and Dave and even Dr. Francis . . . they had not come true. He was not over-reacting to it all. He was just trying to tell me about his boyhood and trying to help me figure out what to do.

"Do you think Dr. Francis was evil?" I asked, feeling like this was one of the most amazing conversations I had ever had with my father and not wanting it to end.

"I know that doctor is sick," he said vehemently. "Who else but a sick man could manipulate kids like that? Because of your mother's influence, I've tried to understand dysfunction and mental illness. I've tried to think scientifically about Hitler and the terrible people in the world, but maybe some people are just evil and that's that."

He turned to look at me again.

"Either way, you know you should tell your mother. She will have better answers for you than I have about sickness and evil."

"I'm not telling her," I shook my head firmly. "It would kill her to know she made me go see that sicko. She will get all messed up if she knows."

Harvey shook his head again, turning back to the road, seeing what I meant and not happy about it.

"We should go back home," I said.

He nodded, put the car in gear, and pulled back onto the highway.

About a mile later, he asked, "Do you have any thoughts, Ben, about how you want to solve the problem of what you did to Allen?" He asked it tentatively or trustingly, like I would have wisdom, but I shook my head. "If you go apologize to Allen, you boys will be arrested," he analyzed, sinking into the problem like I had already done in my head. "The court will put you in juvie, and the Tremmel family would probably try to hurt you themselves. From what you've said about that court case, they are not nice people."

"And we can't get Dave in trouble, either," I pointed out. "The Tremmels would kill Dave if they found out it was him in those white sheets. You and I will leave Durango, but not Dave. He'll be stuck here."

Harvey saw this and nodded his head as he exited the highway at Ninth Street and came to a stoplight.

"We have to think carefully, and I have to figure out if I at least need to talk to Bert about Dave—father to father. Bert is a lawyer, an officer of the court. If I talk to him, will he try to have you arrested? You never know how a father will respond to hearing bad things about his son, but he'd have to arrest his son, too, so I don't think he'd go to the police."

"You can't tell him, Harvey, you know that."

Harvey touched my arm and said, "Ben, I'm sorry that I didn't protect you back then like a father should. Please believe me. I'm sorry. Everything else is confusing, but not that, okay? I did not protect you and I'm sorry."

"It's okay, man. It's okay."

"No, it's not. I didn't protect you from Dr. Francis taking advantage of you. I wasn't around. Your father was gone."

"Dad, it's cool."

Harvey accelerated past the green light at the corner.

"No, let me say this, Ben. You'll be hard on yourself the rest of your life. That's just who you are. I watch you searching through all the world's religions for the single way that's right—Judaism, Christianity, Hinduism, Buddhism, the theater, psychology, everything. They all have meaning, I know that, I poured my heart into them at your age because of opportunity and wisdom in each of them, but I'm not sure they brought me the forgiveness of myself I needed."

I tried to figure out why "forgiveness" should be so important, but Harvey was on a roll again.

"Maybe there's no way to do what's right here in Durango without getting the cops involved, but no matter what, son, you have to realize that thoughts and books about the Self and sweat lodges and smoking dope get you thinking and feeling, but they aren't *life itself*. Being in your head is your way of survival like it is mine and your mom's, but it's also stopping you from finding God and truth and your soul and your Self—all the things and feelings you really want. You got hurt by our divorce and by Dr. Francis and by a tough world and now you're confused. Some of that is my fault, and I know it, but this moment right now, for *you*, Ben, you have to really grab ahold of it."

He made a fist with his right hand.

"Don't be afraid like the rest of us, don't hide. I mean that. Seize this moment. Change your life."

A loud honk sounded from behind our car because Harvey was driving too slowly. We heard a roar and watched a souped-up blue Corvette speed past us on the right. Harvey accelerated back up to the speed limit.

"Do you see what I'm saying, Ben?"

"I guess so."

"It's time to examine your life. Once you go back to New York, you and I won't see each other again for a long time. You'll never spend another summer with me, you'll go to college, you'll make your life without me, but I want to talk to you on the phone more, okay? I want to help."

"Sure," I said automatically as I saw tears reflected on his face again.

The sight immediately grabbed my throat, making my eyes water yet again.

"I'll be okay, Dad."

He turned to me.

"Thank you for calling me Dad." His chin and lip quivered. "I am your dad, even though I've been . . . remiss."

He turned off Florida Road onto Folsom Place, and we went silent, looking at the neighborhood's houses, some dark, some with the blue TV glow in their windows, including Dave's. *Mission Impossible* would be on now.

"What a day," Harvey said as he pulled the car into our driveway, bumping the shallow bottom of the front bumper on the asphalt.

Everything in my life seemed to have collapsed in the last hour or two, but I was still here, getting out of the Dart, looking at the neighborhood.

Harvey and I walked to the front door and stepped inside. I flipped on the light switch, and Harvey followed me to the kitchen.

"I'm sorry I screwed up so bad," I said. "I'm really going to take your advice, Dad. I'll change in the future."

I had no such confidence, nor really knew what it would mean to do that, but I said it anyway.

He seemed more certain. "I know you will," he said, tossing the keys on the kitchen table, putting out his hand, as if we had a new pact.

I shook his hand firmly, and it felt very good.

"Thanks for helping me," I said.

He let go of my hand and reached up to touch my face gently like he did when I was a little boy.

"You bet," he said. "I will always be here for you, as best I can. Remember, son, you are the reason I was born."

# CHAPTER 14

THE NEXT DAY I went down to the hospital. Dave's mom and dad were with him in his room. Bert frowned as he said hello and thanked me for getting Dave there.

"He's not going back out to the Rez, though," he said, "not while he lives in my house. Don't take him out there again."

"Yes, sir," I said instinctively.

His face, very red, allowed nothing but agreement. He was on his way out, carrying a briefcase. I watched him go, then approached Dave's bed. Molly gave me a hug and said, "Dave's fine, all because of you, Ben!"

A memory of Dr. Francis' office in the children's hospital wing flashed through me, but I fought it back and shook Dave's hand. He had an IV hooked to the inside of his left arm.

Molly asked if I would spell her here in the room so she could go out and use the restroom and left us alone for a minute.

Dave whispered, "Thanks for bringing me here, man. Did I say anything in the car? I was pretty out of it, but I remember talking or something."

"In the car, yeah," I nodded, sitting on the edge of the bed down by his feet. "You talked about Allen and that priest, Father Kordash. You didn't make a lot of sense though. It was like you missed him, but you hated him."

"What did I say exactly?" he asked, his eyes boring into mine, his cheeks red.

155

"You mumbled stuff like, 'I don't want to grow up, I won't grow up, Father, I promise.' It sounded like you were dreaming or maybe delirious—that can happen when you're dehydrated, I think."

"Yeah, and what else did I say?"

"You mumbled something like, 'Don't leave.' Kid stuff like that."

"Anything else?"

"Nothing I remember," I said. "Anyways, how are you doing?"

"They're letting him out of the hospital tonight," Molly said, back from the restroom and moving to the beige vinyl chair by the window.

"Cool," I said, "that's cool."

Dave looked out the window, clearly thinking hard about something. I thought about his whispering questions about the car ride and focused on what he said about Father Kordash, which wasn't much, just sadness that his priest, a piano teacher, went away. What was I missing?

I couldn't think about it much more though because Molly talked about how the sweat hadn't worked out but thanked me for being Dave's friend, that I'd been a godsend.

"But why don't you guys spend much time together anymore like you did before?" she asked.

My stomach flipped as I tried to think of something to say.

"It's hard with Ben leaving," Dave answered. "He's got a lot of stuff to do."

"Yeah," I agreed. "I'm out at the Rez all the time up till Friday when I fly back."

This wasn't completely true, as my work at the Rez had completed—just one little party the troupe would throw to say goodbye—but it sounded true and Molly moved on to other thoughts about this fall, Dave's junior year, how smart her baby boy was.

When it was time for me to leave the hospital, Dave waved at me like he wouldn't see me again.

\* \* \*

For the rest of the day I wondered about Father Kordash, turning everything over in my head and stomach. After dinner, I spied on Dave's house from up in my boiling hot bedroom, waiting for him to go out to his fort. When I saw him come out his back door, I rushed downstairs, passing Harvey watching TV, and followed Dave out to the scrublands.

I figured he was going to the fort, but when I got there he had already left or hadn't even gone there at all. Dammit! I doubled back looking for his sneaker prints and found them on a dirt bike trail heading up to the arterial, Florida Road. When I got to Florida Road, I spotted Dave a hundred yards away in his jeans and plaid shirt with his right thumb out trying to catch a ride. In his left fist he clutched a bulging, black garbage bag. I got up onto the shoulder of the road and yelled, "Dave!" He looked around for a moment, and then a dirty gray pickup truck stopped for him. He opened the door, crawled in with his garbage bag, and then rolled away.

*Where was he heading?*

The Lester's place was out the way he headed.

*And what did he have in that bag?*

I ran back home, got the keys to the Dart, and drove to the Lester's place. As I approached, I saw smoke from the distance, so I figured Dave was there. I parked and walked toward the barn. Sure enough, Dave sat in front of a fire, and it looked like he was feeding pages of his journal into it.

"Hey, Dave!" I called.

"Jesus!"

His eyes bugged out, and his face got red.

"Sorry I scared you, man. Didn't you hear me calling you? I called you from the scrublands."

"Ben! What are you doing here? You can't be here!"

"I wanted to talk to you," I said. "There's something going on with you. I don't understand it, but I think you'll feel better if—"

"Get out!" he interrupted, standing up and pointing at the big open barn door.

I moved towards the fire pit, my guts telling me that something big was going on. I saw a Polaroid Dave had taken that night with Allen. *Hadn't we burned those photos?* Dave was about to burn it. "What are you doing? Is that another photo?"

Dave shoved pieces of paper into his jeans pocket and grabbed the photo. "Go away. Now!"

"Are you burning your jour—"

I saw him run at me but couldn't dodge him before getting tackled to the ground. With much more strength than him, I tossed him off and jumped up. He got up and rushed me again. "Dave!" I yelled, stepping aside and swatting him down. "Stop!" He ran at me again, but I caught him and held him in a bear hug. "Calm down! I don't want to hurt you. What's going on?"

Suddenly, he reared back and hit my forehead with his forehead like he had seen on *Baretta*.

"What the hell!" I yelled, not letting go despite the pain.

Dave dropped the papers and wrenched an arm free of the bear hug to punch at me. It didn't do anything except knock both of us to the ground. Dave struggled to get away, but I smashed my elbow into his chest. Anger and adrenalin took over my body, and Dave felt pain and loss of breath immediately.

"Jesus!" I yelled. "What are you doing?"

I jumped up, out of his reach, and grabbed the black booklet. From a football crouch, Dave rushed at me yet again, but I turned, pushed, and then kicked him in the shoulder, knocking him onto his back. "Dave, what is your problem!" On all fours, he scurried toward the two-by-two he had used on Allen.

"You're tripping, man," I yelled. "Tell me what's going on."

Dave rushed me with the board, but this time I'd had enough. I knocked the board away and then hit him in the face, knocking him to the ground. Then I jumped on top of him, my butt on Dave's stomach, my knees pinning his weak arms.

Dave kicked and yelled, but I was too strong.

"Don't read that, Ben," he whined, going from violent to begging in a split second.

"Mellow out!"

"That's my stuff, not yours! Don't read that, please."

I opened the book and began to read a kind of journal-story about Davey and Father Kordash.

"Ben, let me up. I'll be cool. Don't read that."

"Are you . . . what the . . . oh man. The priest? You guys . . . Like Dr. Francis?"

Dave struggled, so I lifted my fist, threatening. "Stop moving!"

I read on, page after page about Little Davey and Father Kordash, his friend, and Father Jerry Brown at the Rez doing things in a sweat lodge. Oh God. It made me want to puke.

"Sorry, man," Dave whined. "I freaked out. Sorry. I won't freak out anymore. You can let me up."

I kept him pinned and read more by going backwards, from right to left like a Hebrew book. I read how Father Kordash taught him piano on the Steinway in the living room like all the kids, but some boys he took down into the basement, and they got naked while playing piano on a flat keyboard synthesizer while they did things. Some days Davey bent over a table while Father Kordash raped him, and one day without telling the parents, Father Kordash drove Dave out to the Rez, where the little boy gave Father Brown a blow job while Father Kordash spoke Latin to Dave while he went inside his rectum.

"Oh man, Dave. You and the priest . . . inside your . . . Oh man."

I jumped off Dave and tottered away, feeling like I was going to fall over.

"He cornholed you!" I yelled, the sound echoing through the barn. "You were eleven? That priest, he . . . you liked it . . . and now you're . . . what . . . what?"

I shook my head at it all, things I had never seen before. "You wanted me all summer. That's why I was your friend, even though you're so dorky?" I asked hoarsely. "Is that it? It's not just that you're smart or that I had empathy and sympathy, whatever, but it's this stuff, your erections. You want me. You want guys now, but you're confused. And the stuff with Allen, that extra stuff . . . you wanted to do . . . no, wait . . . I don't get it . . . are you . . ."

"No, no, I'm not," Dave panted with his pale zitty face and long arms gesturing, trying to get control. "Ben, it's just a story, man. I know it's weird, but I started writing it after you talked about not wanting to get cornholed if you went to jail for protesting the Vietnam war, remember? While we were driving out to the Rez? You said that. Then when you told me about Dr. Francis, I wrote this whole story. Man, Ben, Father Kordash didn't do all that stuff to me. Are you kidding? I just got the story in my head after you told me about Dr. Francis. I like girls, man."

I stood frozen there, my mind trying to work. *Father Brown. The Rez.*

"Dave, this is way bad. He cornholed you. How many times, man? This is a big deal. This is, like, trauma to your brain, man. These guys are evil. Like Dr. Francis. I've been thinking a lot about this stuff since the night with Allen. This is evil, man. This is sick."

Dave touched his aching cheek and moved his jaw.

"It's not what you think. It's imagination." He was speaking calmly now, getting control. "You told me about Dr. Francis, and I knew more stuff happened to you with Dr. Francis than you told me. I guessed Dr. Francis did this stuff with you, and that's when the story just started in my head. I'm a writer, man. I'm an artist. Stories just get in my head and I write them. You know how that is, right? I mean, I know it's a freaky story. I've got a freaky imagination, but none of this happened. I just need to get laid, that's all."

"Jesus!" My fists kept clenching harder and harder. "All summer everyone said stuff about you being depressed or something—your mom, my dad, my mom. But I was blind. Why was I blind? I was—"

"I'm cool," Dave interrupted. "The truth is, you told me you were telling me the truth about Dr. Francis, but it's you whose brain is messed up by that doctor, not me. I imagined a whole story because I could tell from your voice that the doctor did more to you than you said, so I wrote it in a story and pretended Father Kordash was, like, Dr. Francis. Ben, this stuff happened to you, not me. You sucked him and got cornholed, not me."

"No way! That shrink never cornholed me, man!"

"Yeah, but you gave him blow jobs and he gave you blow jobs. I wanted to be your friend all the way, your best friend. But you don't know how to be a friend, not really. You just lie all the time and pretend to be cool, like pretending you've been laid when you haven't. You're not cool, you're not a big brother. You're a screw-up who lies to feel better. At least I'm honest and told you everything about Allen, but now you're gonna lie to me and say nothing big happened with Dr. Francis, but I know he did all this stuff to you."

"No way, man! No way!" I hissed, confused. "Dr. Francis made me give him some blow jobs, and yeah, he blew me a few times, but that's it. He didn't cornhole me, for God's sake. You can't blame this on me. It was you who wanted to do the bad stuff to Allen. Not me."

And right then I saw the world become better again for Dave in his weird eyes even before I understood why, and I opened up my mouth in silent shock as I realized I had just told Dave the secret I didn't want anyone to know.

I reached my hands up and pulled at my hair with both hands. "You . . . you just got into my head!" I shrieked. "I didn't understand . . . I'm sorry . . . you got it so much worse than me. That priest did it so much worse to you . . . and now I just told you about the blow jobs."

"Yes. I know your secret now," Dave said, smiling, cold and calm. "From now on, I own you—you better be very careful."

"How was I so stupid?" I yelled into the air. "Since the night here with Allen I thought I groked what was up with you, with me, but I didn't understand anything. I'm never saying 'grok' again. It's a stupid word! Everything's messed up. I'm . . . I just can't understand anything."

Turning away from him, I looked up at the sun coming in the big door of the barn, barely knowing where I was.

"You can hit me," Dave said. "You'll feel better. Guys always feel better when they hit me."

"I'm not gonna hit you. Jesus!" I started to move away from him, wanting to get out of here. "Look, you gotta talk to your dad, Dave. You got to. It's definite. You're psychologically a mess, man. You need help. If you don't talk to him, I will."

"No, you won't," Dave said, completely sure of himself. "You're the one who's messed up, not me. You're the one who went to the shrink, not me. I'm cool, man. I can fly and be happy way beyond you, you stupid freak."

He breathed in deeply, loudly, like he had just solved everything.

I didn't know what he meant by "fly" but hissed again. "You better talk to someone, or I will. I mean it."

Again, Dave shook his head, as if talking to a child.

"I won't say anything about a stupid story, and you won't either, because if you do tell anyone about this story, I'll tell your blow job secret to your dad and I'll call your mom in New York. Everyone will know your secret, including your mom, who'll feel so bad about sending you to Dr. Francis. Think about that, Benny. Do you want her to know how messed up you are because of her?"

My mouth hung open, but no words came out.

I had to get away.

I turned and ran out the barn door so fast I tripped, got up again, and kept running.

When I got to the Dart, I slammed my fist on the car top and screamed at the blue sky like an animal howling in rage.

Then I yanked my door open, got in, cranked the engine, pushed the accelerator hard, and spit gravel as I sped away.

# CHAPTER 15

"DID THE PRIEST REALLY DO THAT stuff to Dave?" I asked the black asphalt and the brown hay and the blue mountain peaks as I gripped the sheepskin cover of the steering wheel.

"Could a priest do that?"

*If doctors could, priests could.*

Father Kordash in Dave's story did everything to the boy that Dr. Francis did with me, but much more, and he made Dave do stuff to his friend in a sweat lodge on the Rez, which was why Dave knew what a sweat lodge looked like! And Father Kordash had sex with a little boy—Dave—lots of times. This meant Dave wanted to do crazy weird stuff to Allen because Father Kordash had done it to him. That must be the psychology of it, right? Did I now understand why he and I had become friends—because there was something freaky about us both?

This made me shudder, and I remembered how little I was, such a tiny boy, so afraid Dr. Francis would cornhole me because he liked putting his finger inside me when he sucked on me and talked about other things he could do. I had become terrified of Dr. Francis when he said, "You know, my penis could go inside your beautiful little anus. Did you know that?"

*Dave must have been so scared, so scared.*

"I gotta get out of this place!" I screamed, gunning the accelerator and passing a farmer in his slow pickup.

I had thought a lot about what my father said, about how I had to change some things. I wanted to do the right thing, only the right thing. Was "the right thing" more than getting out of town and not letting my mother know the worst stuff? Was the "right thing" to help Dave somehow?

Maybe Dave was mentally screwed up now, but Judith said every teenager could be treated, everyone was curable. What about that? What had Dave done, after all? He'd only done a bad thing to Allen so far, right?

And wait a minute, I thought suddenly. Maybe I was freaking out. Maybe it was all part of Dave's imagination like he'd said. Hadn't I joked with Harvey and Dave in the car on the way to the Rez one time about how, if I had been old enough to be drafted, it would have been better to resist the draft and get cornholed in jail than go die in Vietnam? Yes, so maybe Dave didn't really get cornholed by Father Kordash. Maybe, like Dave said, he decided to put what I'd said into a story. Maybe Dave was just a gay kid, and it all got jumbled together inside his imagination.

Really?

No way.

Even just imagining sex with a man and a boy wasn't right. Sex between men was different—but a man and a little *boy*. Dave knew all that Latin and that Father Kordash had been a priest.

But wait a minute—could this priest do all this stuff to Dave when he was a little boy without anyone knowing? Molly seemed very into all the piano stuff, and she loved Father Kordash. There was no way Dave could have been cornholed by Father Kordash without anyone knowing.

But why not? No one knew about Dr. Francis and me.

Still, maybe Dave somehow guessed about me and the blow jobs with Dr. Francis and put that in the story too.

No no no.

Yes.

Maybe.

No!

*Why the hell did I just admit to the blow jobs to Dave?*

Dave was freaky, he always was a misfit, and every once in a while, like earlier in the Lester's barn, his eyes lost their gold flecks and just looked cold. When that happened, Dave looked like a completely weirdo kid, as mean as Allen, or meaner. This is what his eyes must have looked like deep in that hood when he forced Allen to beat off in the sawdust, with the gun at his butt.

*Why did I like Dave? What had I seen in him all summer?*

*Why had my father even introduced us? Thanks, Harvey!*

And what about the pact? But wait a minute. Think about Allen. There was still another option. Maybe Dave didn't reveal to me everything about what Allen did to him, think about that. Maybe Allen cornholed Dave when Dave was a boy. And maybe that's why Dave wanted to do it with Allen and the gun. Not because of Father Kordash but Allen? Maybe all those bad things Dave wanted to do to Allen were in his head because he could feel in his soul that Allen had turned him into a freak and . . .

"Where the hell am I?" I asked myself.

I looked around and pulled onto the shoulder of the rural road as a truck passed and hit me with wind. I was well past the turn into Durango. I had accidentally gone west toward Cortez and Mesa Verde National Park.

"Get control, Ben. Figure things out."

Another truck buffeted the Dart as it passed, and I clicked on the radio, heard Bachman Turner Overdrive play "Takin' Care of Business," and twisted the dial to another station. Pink Floyd sang "Money." I twisted the dial to another station and heard a song by Hank Williams. I clicked the dial to "off" and looked back over my shoulder for traffic. When I had the chance, I pulled onto the road and accelerated in a U turn, heading back into the mountains.

"I won't ever see or speak to Dave again," I said to the sun on the car's hood. "I'm leaving. Today was goodbye."

But I had to be very careful with Dave and the adults. Dave and I had to at least pretend to get along for the next three days. If we didn't, wouldn't the adults grill us like Molly tried to? Then we'd have to explain something, wouldn't we? And didn't I have to pretty much stay on Dave's good side? If I didn't, he could tell Harvey about Dr. Francis and the blow jobs. He didn't know Harvey knew some stuff already, but if I acted weird or Dave learned that I broke the pact, he would get revenge on me by calling my mom. That was for sure. Look what he did to Allen. By now, twenty minutes later, Dave would have burnt the story, so I would have no proof of anything about him. *Dammit! If only I had kept some of that story!* Okay. But what proof would Dave have that I had given Dr. Francis the blow jobs either? And where was Dave's journal? If only I had that. Dave had burned a black book, not the blue spiral notebook I'd seen in the fort that first day in Durango. And what about the bruise around Dave's eye? Dave would have to tell his mom he fell, not that he and I fought, because if he told her we fought, his parents would come to me and I would tell on Dave about Father Kordash, though without proof.

Dammit.

Thank God Harvey would leave this town in a few weeks. He was hitting the road with the theater troupe, all their gigs in New Mexico, Arizona and California. The Brickmans could get out of Durango clean. If Dave and I didn't act too abnormal, and if we said a quick goodbye in the next three days so the parents didn't suspect anything, then that would be the end of it. Right? And there was no way to help Dave any more than I'd already tried. No safe way. But—*dammit*—should I help him more? Was I still supposed to be a good friend and try to help this messed up kid? Should I talk to his father or ask Harvey to talk to Bert?

I kept thinking and thinking with my window wide open, wind hitting me, my misty eyes drying out. I drove alongside the narrow-gauge railroad tracks that disappeared as the road climbed farther up the blue and green mountains. "What does a man do?" I asked the mountains. Does a man risk his own mom knowing about Dr. Francis? Does a man reveal to the adults everything about Dave? And what is "everything?" I didn't know. And what if Mrs. McConnell calls Mom and tells her about Dr. Francis and the blow jobs, and Mom can't forgive herself for insisting I go to Dr. Francis every week, and then my mother and I can't be like we are anymore? What if she couldn't forgive herself? Harvey talked about forgiveness. Why did I love my mother so much? Why did I care so much if she found out? Why did I have to feel "so protective of her," like my father said?

Passing a ranch on my right, I saw a blue wagon wheel jutting up out of the grassy meadow like a sculpture. Next to the wagon wheel sat an old rusted covered wagon from a hundred years ago. Past the wagon was a green late model Plymouth, its grill facing a blue house, the last house I saw as I drove further upward toward the mountain peaks.

I remembered looking up at the mountains my first day in Durango, before I followed Dave into the scrublands. I remembered joking with Dave in those first weeks about how there were monks or medicine men on the mountain tops, praying and meditating up there, making the mountain tops seem blue. A sign appeared on my right, reading, "Scenic Overlook, One Mile Ahead." I slowed down, hoping there would be a phone booth and seeing one next to a low building with restrooms. I pulled into the parking lot and saw a family looking through a telescope at the overlook ledge.

"I want my mommy," I heard in my head as I remembered the final time that I saw Dr. Francis, terrified when my mother picked me up at his door. She had taken my hand, guiding me to the elevator, asking, "How'd it go?"

"Great," I'd said, squeezing her hand, so happy I was safe with her, ready to negotiate with her that I would be a very good boy so I didn't have to go back there to see the doctor anymore.

I stepped out of the Dart, looked down at the mountain valley. The air was colder here than in town, and my naked arms and knees and calves were chilling with goosebumps. Voices of the tourist family carried on the wind, their words garbled. I avoided looking at them, moving to the phone booth where I took a quarter from my pocket, put it into the slot, got the operator, and asked her to make a collect call to New York. My mother didn't answer so we hung up. What would she be doing right now, so late at night in New York? Shouldn't she have been asleep? It was almost midnight there.

Stepping out of the phone booth, I moved toward the edge of a low rock wall. The tourist mom in a yellow windbreaker pulled her little daughter back from leaning against the rock wall, pointing out how dangerous the low rocks were, especially with such strong wind. I moved away from them and leaned over the wall where I could see to the steep embankment hundreds of feet below. "Just fall," I whispered to myself. I would end everything by leaning forward. When I fell, I would fall into God's big hand that always pulled at me when I came to high places. I would fall into a huge light all around me, then I would become that beautiful light. Spreading my arms like wings, I murmured, "Let's fly." The cold mountain air enveloped my arms and torso and legs with coldness, but I felt a terrible, weird, happy urge to be completely free, to just finish it all right now.

And right then, as if for no reason at all, Allen Tremmel came into my mind—not Allen naked in the barn, but Allen playing piano in his father's store. Closing my eyes tight, focusing, I saw

Dave's story about the boy and Father Kordash in my head and remembered a time during surveillance of Allen when Dave and I saw him playing the piano in the window at the Tremmel's furniture store. Dave said somewhere early in our plan-making that Allen's family was Catholic, and Allen used to take piano lessons from Father Kordash. And in the store window, Allen's fingers had moved fast, his face bent into the piano. His hands moved on the piano like Dave's hands did.

"Oh God!"

Allen was two years older. Father Kordash had been Allen's teacher before he had been Dave's teacher. Father Kordash had done things to Dave, so maybe he had done things to Allen.

Wind hit my sweaty body, and I wrapped my arms around my chest and grabbed my shoulders for warmth.

Maybe Allen hated Dave and tried to do bad things to Dave because of Father Kordash. Dave thought that all of Allen's meanness toward him came from the lawsuit, but in Dave's story, Father Kordash hinted that Dave would one day not come back and then Father Kordash left. Wouldn't Father Kordash have told Allen not to come back too? What if Allen had been a little boy who loved Father Kordash, just like Dave did? Now he hated Dave. Jesus! It was twisted, but what if—

"Hey son!" came a voice to my left.

I opened my eyes as a man in brown polyester pants and a blue windbreaker walked briskly toward me.

"Hey son, that doesn't look safe."

Startled by his voice and tall body next to me, I pulled back from the rock wall and the cliff's edge.

"Yeah," I said as I walked away, back to the car where I leaned against the Dart.

If what I had just realized was right, then Ben Brickman was different from Allen and Dave. I didn't want to do to other people what Dr. Francis did to me, not to anyone. I had a twisted mind that could imagine anything bad and was like a soldier always on guard, so yes, I was messed up, but I wasn't evil like Allen—and Dave—seemed to be.

I got back into my car, shivering but very happy, and turned the heater on. It rattled as it started up. Looking at the edge of the mountain just outside the car window, I murmured, "Was I gonna jump? No way." But as the car warmed, and I rubbed my arms and legs with my palms, I thought I could have. Then I thought about Eagleclaw again. He had said something about bad things on the Rez, something about his son. Did it involve Father Jerry Brown? No way, that would be too much of a coincidence, but what had he meant? Was it something similar to what happened to Dave?

I turned on the radio, listened to the Beatles' "Hey Jude" then Yes' "Roundabout." When I arrived at the rural fields and farms just outside Durango, there was a Winnebago turned on its side so traffic had stopped and cops were everywhere, directing traffic to go back. I followed other cars down a bunch of rural roads I had never been on, an alternative route to Durango.

When I got back to the town, I went straight to the Tremmel's furniture store and pulled over across the street. I stared at the pianos in the window, trying to confirm my insights, analyzing, still not knowing what to do. After about five minutes, I drove back out onto Florida Road. Pulling over to the shoulder just before Folsom Place, I turned the car off, found a piece of paper in the glove compartment and the pencil that we had used to clean out the gun. It still had a bit of a burn smell to it.

I started writing a letter to the McConnells.

*Dear Mr. and Mrs. McConnell,*
*I don't know where to start, but I didn't know anything about any of this when I met Dave that day in the scrublands. Now, I'm*

*just trying to do the right thing, I promise. I'm really sorry. I'm really
really sorry . . ."*

I wrote everything down that I could think was safe to write—
about Allen, Father Kordash, Dave. When I finished, I read it over
and over and thought it was okay—but it scared me. Giving it to
the McConnells would explode everything. "Give it to them after
you leave Durango," I mumbled to myself, thinking about Dave's
fort, about Jerry Brown's sweat lodge, and realizing something
suddenly.

"Oh man," I yelled inside the car, "Oh man, am I too late?"

I turned the ignition, the starter squealing like it always did,
and raced back home.

# CHAPTER 16

"I'VE GOT TO GET OUT to the scrublands," I said quickly to Harvey, who was working at the kitchen table.

He tapped at his typewriter, concentrating, and said, "It's getting pretty dark, so be safe."

I left the keys to the Dart on top of some scripts on the table and raced out the back door with a flashlight. Running through the now familiar trails, I got to the debris piles and boulders and climbed up and over.

No music played. The fort was empty.

Thinking about Father Brown, something clicked in my head. I clawed with my fingers underneath the area that would, in a sweat lodge, be the rock pit. Dave might have already come back here, if he could hitch back in time, but maybe I beat him. If so, I would find his journal right here. I dug fast, my fingers, hands, arms, legs covered in dirt.

A foot below the surface, I felt plastic.

Pulling up a big white kitchen bag with both hands, I saw the spiral notebook, a flashlight, the transistor radio, a shoe string, *Absalom, Absalom* by William Faulkner, the Polaroid of Allen getting hit, and the plastic hospital tag not of Dave McConnell but of someone named Philip McKenzie. It made sense. Dave would have been in the sweat lodge with Jerry Brown and Father Kordash. He knew about the rock pit inside a sweat lodge. He built his fort like a sweat lodge and instead of building a rock pit, he hid his stuff underground where the rock pit would be.

Why was this stash still here? I didn't know, but I knew I was lucky. Covering the hole with dirt again, wanting to get clear of the fort before Dave came back, I crawled out, pulled the flap back down, and listened for anything suspicious.

I crawled over the boulder and came down the other side running far off trail.

I stopped and listened.

Still no one.

Running deeper into the scrublands, I found a place hidden from view and sat down in the weedy dried grass to open the spiral notebook.

"From the Library of David McConnell," in careful cursive, fit onto the center of the first page.

Underneath that Dave had written, "For Father Kordash, wherever you are."

"Oh man," I mumbled, afraid of what I would read.

I flipped through the journal, saw some pages gone—perhaps burnt in the fire at Lester's, or perhaps the pages he smashed into his pockets—yet a lot remained. I couldn't stop myself from reading.

In an entry for June 16, Dave depicted the day at the lagoon in careful detail.

In another entry, he depicted our meeting.

He carefully wrote the plan to get me involved in helping him hurt Allen.

He wrote speculations of scenes and scripts in which we did much more to Allen than we had, including Dave pushing the gun deep into Allen, then firing it.

"Oh Dave," I moaned in the dirt, wanting to tear this book apart, wanting to puke, but reading on.

Dave wrote that his plan for "destroying Allen" would work with me involved, but he couldn't spend the night with me—except for part of one night when he would fake being asleep—because his mom had heard him talking in his sleep a couple months ago when she walked by his room to go to the bathroom. "I'm so sorry Father Kordash left you," she had said the next morning, and he grilled her about anything else he had said, and she said, "Just that you missed him." On that day he decided to fake falling asleep with me and mumble about Allen. "Ben will do whatever I want him to, within reason," he wrote. "He thinks he's smart, the big brother, but he's so gullible!"

Jesus!

Finding a page that described my confession to him about Dr. Francis, he wrote, "Now I have Ben trapped, and he will help me. I will gain the confidence I need from the night in the barn and then will not need Ben anymore. I will miss him, but he's just a stupid kid who thinks he's brave. I'm the brave one now." Was Dave trying to make me like Kordash made Father Brown?

Flipping through more pages, I stopped randomly at various days, piecing together the story I had begun to suspect up at the scenic overlook.

Allen's family was Catholic just like Dave's, Allen an acolyte just like Dave who took piano lessons from Father Kordash. Allen hated Dave because Allen had been Father Kordash's favorite, really great at piano, the star of his family and the priest's best and special friend. But then Dave came along and took that away. Turning pages, I read what little Davey and Father Kordash did together, how it started, how much Dave loved Father Kordash and played piano for him while Father Kordash touched him. When they did these things together, they would use the synthesizer piano in Father Kordash's basement, in a locked room the house cleaner, Mrs. Albott, and no other priest was allowed into. Dave wrote, "When I feel worried or down, I go walk by Father Kordash's house and feel better. One day I need a house like that with a room like that. Until then, I will have my fort. Maybe one day soon I can bring a boy there."

Tears came to my eyes, and I had to turn away from that page.

When I was able to continue, I read about how Father Kordash had suddenly been forced to leave town, like he had gotten into trouble for something. "I believed if I never grew hair," Dave wrote, "he would never stop loving me. Maybe I will never grow hair, ever, and maybe I'll find him somewhere, and we can be together."

"Jesus!" I hissed at Dave's careful cursive.

Vomit rose, so I turned quickly and puked on all fours into the weeds. When it had all come out, I puked nothing more than bile, tears in my eyes. Now I understood the weird confused feeling that made you want to die sometimes, of liking the very feelings you hated, and I felt I had to read more. I got my head together, flipped through more of the journal, and read an entry from yesterday about what happened in the sweat lodge, how Dave had been worried all summer about doing a sweat but then started "doing those good things at the hospital," and decided that "being brave" meant going into the sweat lodge to see the other naked kids there.

I flipped the pages back to earlier entries, trying to find what he meant by "doing those good things at the hospital." I found it on August 10. Dave described going to the hospital with his mother to visit their old church friend, Mr. Ostheller, a man who had taught Dave how to play chess and who was dying from cancer. These visits occurred after I had told him the story of Dr. Francis, he wrote, and my story about Dr. Francis gave him an idea.

"I don't want to be a priest, so I think I will be a doctor," Dave wrote. "I think that is another 'meant to be' about knowing Ben."

In three different journal entries after August 10, Dave described the thrill of visiting a nine-year-old boy, Philip McKenzie, in a coma in the pediatric wing. Dave described closing the door behind him, walking to the boy's bed, lifting the sheets, and playing with the comatose boy's genitals.

"Oh God!"

My yell into the scrublands echoed, or at least I thought it did, so loud, so confused and angry.

I lifted back onto all fours and puked out waves of yellow bile.

My ribs felt like they were breaking.

For several moments, I thought it would never stop—that I would die.

When I sat back down on my butt, I dried my eyes with the back of my hand and realized I had to destroy this book. On the other hand, if I burned it, this sick boy's life would become private again, and invisible. No one would ever read it or see it, because there were no plays or movies or books about this stuff. No one talked about this.

But I had to burn it.

Yes.

It was sick.

I pulled my Bic lighter out of my pocket and set fire to the pages, dropped the flaming book onto my vomit, and stepped away to watch smoke rise. As it burned, I threw the shoelace and flashlight into the fire, and the radio, and the Polaroid Dave must have switched out that night at the Lester's barn. Within minutes, everything except the metal spirals of the notebook and parts of the radio and flashlight had burned up.

To Dave, I said aloud, "I'm sorry, man. I don't understand everything, but I'm sorry."

He didn't answer, of course. In the quiet of the forest, I stood there watching the fire and thinking about my mother.

I would tell her everything, I decided. I had to tell her. She was a psychologist, she could help me understand. It was right to tell her. I had to do the right thing.

When I got back to the house, it was long after dark. I found my father sitting at his kitchen table working at his typewriter. He was clearly relieved to see me, his face looking very worried.

"Thank God, Ben. There you are. Thank God."

"What's up?" I asked.

"It's Dave. He's run away. His folks can't find him. He left a note. He said no one will ever see him again."

"Whoa."

"Bert told me his note said, 'Ben will know why. Ben should not have taken what was not his.' What does that mean, Ben?"

"Oh man!"

I sat down to think. Something had kept Dave from going back to his fort and getting the journal. He went to visit Father Kordash's old house, I thought. Or maybe he didn't think I would find his stash, or maybe he went to the hospital. Whatever he did, he must have later gone back to the fort, right after I was there, seen the hole dug up and the journal gone, and panicked.

I sat there trembling next to my father.

"Ben, you're pale. What's going on?"

I told my father everything that had happened, the fight with Dave at the Lester's place, what I realized about Allen, writing the letter, going to the fort, finding the journal, what I read, what I saw, the shoelace and the Polaroid, Dave at the hospital with Philip McKenzie.

"Ben," my father kept whispering. "Oh dear. Oh no."

He didn't say it, but a part of him wished I had kept the journal so there was proof.

So did I.

"What do we tell the McConnells?" he asked me, the room, the house, the air. "What do we do? You're right, he must have run away because you found his journal."

What we decided was simple. We would tell the McConnells we didn't know what Dave meant. I would go back to New York, but not before writing everything down for the McConnells in a letter. My father would hold onto this complete letter until he left town, at which time he would give the letter to Molly and Bert. By then, maybe Dave would have come home. In fact, maybe he would come home tonight or tomorrow, but either way, we would avoid contact with Dave. At the same time, we had to act normal.

Walking over to the McConnells, joining in the search for Dave, we told them we thought Dave must have meant that he was ashamed and embarrassed about what happened at the sweat lodge. They were worried and frantic and didn't stop to question us much, and at about 2:00 a.m., we came home to go to bed.

\* \* \*

Two days later, Dave still hadn't returned, and it was time for me to go back to New York. We put my big brown trunk in the car and drove to the airport. I sat with my arm out the window catching the breeze, remembering a long drive with my parents from New York to Chicago when I was five.

*"Look! It's a dragon!" I'd said, pointing at a cloud.*

*"No way, it's a lion," Daddy laughed.*

*"I think it's a peanut," Mommy smiled.*

*"A peanut?" I giggled. "No way!"*

"Remember when we used to name the cloud-animals?" I asked my father.

"I remember," my father smiled. "I'll miss you, Ben."

"Thanks, Dad. I'll miss you."

"And call me anytime, okay son. I'm so sorry about everything."

"It's cool, Dad. It's okay."

At the curb outside the United Airlines gate, we got out of the car, and I looked at his long graying ponytail and thought about cutting my hair before school started. He helped me get my trunk down to the curb, and I pulled my backpack on. We lifted the trunk onto a cart, rolled it into the airport, and got my ticket.

When my flight was called, I hugged my father and said, "I love you, man."

He whispered, "I love you too, son."

My eyes watered, and so did his. Then I turned and gave my ticket to the woman in the United Airlines uniform and walked out onto the tarmac, up the ladder, and into the plane where I had to bow my head through the doorway and all the way to my seat, 8D.

I put my backpack on my lap, looked out the window toward the flat airport building as the pilot started the propeller. The stewardess came through the aisle telling me to stow my backpack under the seat and put on my seatbelt. When the plane started moving, I spotted my father waving at me, and I waved back.

The plane taxied onto the runway, paused, accelerated, rose into the air, then veered left along the ridge of the Rocky Mountains. When it turned to fly northeast, I looked down at the mesas and desert below.

There's the Rez, I thought.

Yesterday, Eagleclaw had hugged me goodbye, saying, "I will always remember you, Ben." I hadn't known how to ask him about Jerry Brown, so I didn't.

Pulling *The Teachings of Don Juan* out of my backpack, I opened up dog-eared pages, then closed the book.

I had done things in Durango I would never have thought I

could do. I wasn't a Fantasarian anymore. In a normal senior year, a guy could be lazy, not go to class as much as before, hang out more. I didn't want to do that.

I took *Siddhartha* out of my backpack, looking at its front cover with the Buddha on it. I wondered whether I had done the right thing by writing the letter that told Dave's parents everything, including everything Father Kordash had done to him. Then I rehearsed what I would say to my mother—everything that Harvey and I knew needed to be said.

In Denver, I transferred to a jet to La Guardia, fell asleep on the way, then woke up as we were landing in New York. When I walked off the plane, it was eight o'clock in the evening, air still hot, much more humid than Durango, so that beads of sweat popped onto my forehead immediately. My mom spotted me and rushed over in her colorful blouse and blue jeans for a hug, her eyes watery. She smelled strongly of cigarettes, the top of her head only reaching up to my chest.

"Hi Mom," I smiled. "It sure is good to be home."

We stepped back from each other, and I saw she had more tiny hairs growing out of her chin like black fuzz. The normal round bags that held her naturally brown eyes seemed a little darker than before. Her teeth were browner than two months ago, but that was beautiful to me.

"Let me look at you!" she grinned, still holding my biceps.

"I'm like the stone boy," I said. "Reunited with his mother."

Her eyes showed she didn't know who the stone boy was, so I explained Eagleclaw's story to her as my luggage came out the chute.

"You've grown so much!" she shook her head in amazement. "I bet you're a full inch taller!"

"Sure, Mom."

"Tell me everything, Ben. How did it end up with your father and Eagleclaw and Dave?"

"Wow, that's a long story," I smiled carefully, "but can I wait on that? Tell me what's happening here first, okay?"

Excited, she didn't bother to counteract my diversion, and when we got back to the apartment by cab, Mom paid the driver who helped us unload the huge trunk, and then we went up the elevator.

For a split second, nothing mattered but the sights and smells of our apartment.

The living room smelled like Mom's tobacco and the lavender potpourri she put in the bathroom, bedroom, and kitchen.

Her Olivetti typewriter and books and journals and stacks of paper sat on the north half of the wooden dining room table.

She had set two places for dinner on the other half.

She had even put out her mother's fancy china and silverware.

I saw the windows, the brown couch, the coffee table, chairs, cabinets, family pictures, paintings, a blue and white rubbing from an English church, a Picasso print, a nude woman by Titian.

Throughout the apartment were bookshelves filled with Mom's hundreds of books.

I realized I was starving and asked, "What's for dinner?"

"What else?" she smiled, opening a pot lid so I could smell it.

"Beef stroganoff?"

"Of course! Your favorite. Now go get unpacked while I heat it up and make the noodles. But at dinner, I want to hear everything about Durango. Don't hold anything back."

"Sure. You're the best, Mom," I smiled, keeping up the good cheer, my stomach roiling in nausea. Could I really tell her everything? Could I? I had to.

In my room I found everything the same as I had left it, Led

Zeppelin and Supertramp posters on my wall, my single bed still made, my grandmother's homemade quilt still lying on the bed with its red and green squares, a major source of laughter when Jeremy and I sat in there getting stoned, trying to count the squares but laughing because we just couldn't concentrate enough to finish. I wondered if I should call Jeremy immediately. No, not tonight.

Would I tell Jeremy about Dave?

No. That would be too weird to explain.

Outside my open window, sparrows chirped in the remaining daylight. A truck rumbled by. Red dusk reflected off the windows of Jeremy's building across the street, a red glare on the glass. I walked to my window and looked out, saw a flock of sparrows like a brown net dropping onto the branches of the tiny elm tree that grew out of the sidewalk below.

"Hey, Mom, where're the headphones?" I called to her.

"Oh yes, here."

I grabbed the new headphones she had bought me as a gift, headphones she warned me on the phone could "ruin my eardrums so you must be careful, okay?" Okay, I had said, and now I put them on as I unpacked my stuff. In my trunk was an album my father had gotten me as a going away present, *Born to Run*, by a new guy from New Jersey named Bruce Springsteen. On the album cover, the bearded Springsteen smiled and leaned against a big black guy who was playing saxophone.

I put the album on my turntable, and the long chord of the headphones strung from one side of the room to the other as I tried to memorize the lyrics and sing along while unpacking my clothes and albums and books. Out of the corner of my eye, I saw some dusk glare on the windows becoming a deeper red. Taking the headphones off, I walked out to the vertical sliding window just off the living room, crawled through the window and out onto the fire escape.

Without the music, I was aware again of my clutching, nervous, painful stomach. Gripping the metal rail, I gazed at the windows across the street that were now like red and purple mirrors, Jeremy's window on the far left. A taxi horn bleated. Archie Bunker's laugh track blared out from a television in a window below. A barge sounded its horn on the river just past NYU's Medical School. Far above me, the reddish streaks of clouds were becoming yellow, like long pieces of gold yarn that bulged in their middles.

I thought of my father's gold kitchen, how Mom, Dad, and I made fun of it, and I thought about Dave's story at the Lester's barn, how Dave and his mother drove in the snow to Father Kordash's house for piano lessons. I closed my eyes and remembered my own winter days when I was ten years old, how I used to come outside right here and grip the black metal, wishing my father were not gone. My mommy bundled me in my blue coat and black cap and purple mittens to take me to Dr. Francis. She was sad all the time, but she took my hand into hers, our shoes sloshing through the snow down Lexington and up 18th. Then into the vestibule, up the loud, humming elevator, and into a warm office. My mother pulled my mittens off my little hands, and I took my own coat off, certain I had been evil or very bad.

'It'll be all right,' my mother had said. 'The doctor will help you.'

From outside the apartment, I heard the phone ring.

I walked back inside and said, "I bet that's dad."

"Checking up to make sure you made it safe, huh?"

"Kind of," I nodded. The phone rang a third time as my mother lifted the receiver and said, "Hello."

Immediately she nodded, letting me know it was Harvey.

I saw the salad bowl and dinner rolls on the table and our water glasses filled up. I could see the stroganoff finished on the stove, the burner off, the noodles steaming in a ceramic bowl just near my place at the table.

Harvey was my back up. We had agreed he would call me to make sure I talked to my mother.

"Sure, here he is," Mom said, and gave me the phone.

"Did you tell her yet?" he asked.

"I'll tell her right now."

My mom took the phone back and put it on its cradle, not even saying goodbye to Harvey. "Tell me what?" she asked, sitting down at the table to ladle out some food.

"Well," I said, eating some beef stroganoff, really wanting it, but so queasy I had to push my chair back.

"What, Ben?"

It took me a lot of breathing and hoping and talking inside myself to be brave as my mom asked, "What's going on? What, Ben?" before I finally did tell her.

I withheld nothing about Dr. Francis and what I did to him on my knees.

I withheld nothing about how scared I felt and how scared I had been for seven years.

I withheld nothing about how I held the gun on Allen and froze when Dave did weird things to him.

I withheld nothing from Mom about how I was not the "new man" she wanted me to be—perfect and kind all the time, never thinking violent thoughts.

"Mom, I hated you for making me go see Dr. Francis," I told her. "I love you, but that's the truth."

When I finished talking, she was crying, and I was crying. "Oh God, Ben. I'm so sorry."

"I know," I murmured.

She could barely talk, and I didn't know what else to say.

She grabbed me in her little hands and arms and sighed, holding me against her tiny body.

"Ben, please don't cry. It was my fault. I didn't know. Oh Ben, it was all my fault."

"No, it wasn't," I said, trying to comfort her the best I could. We were lost for a long time together there, completely lost.

Finally, my mom said, "My God, Ben, that is the bravest thing I think a man has ever done in my life, telling me all of that. I am so proud of you, Ben."

I have remembered those words my whole life.

# AFTERWORD

IF I AM KNOWN AT ALL, it is probably for *The Wonder of Boys,
The Wonder of Girls,* or another nonfiction work in the fields of
education or psychology. If you have read any of my work in
applied neuroscience and psychology—or even my less-known
novels and poetry—you will know of my hopefulness about
human nature, but also my vigilance against its dark side.

I started writing *The Stone Boys* in college four decades ago,
feeling certain of only one thing—that I wanted to write it in a
voice and style that not only adults but also adolescents of twelve
and older would appreciate. It has taken me this long to complete
and publish this book not only because the voice and story needed
extreme care, but also because my own emotional responses kept
rising and falling with memories as I wrote.

Some of this book is autobiographical. At ten, like Ben, I was
molested by my psychiatrist. Ben's story is almost exactly mine, as
is Ben's escape, though my escape happened before the oral sex not
after. Gail, my wife, did a Google search recently and discovered
that my psychiatrist was later prosecuted for crimes against other
boys, and two years ago, facing new prosecution and prison time,
shot himself. Reading that news report, I felt no elation, nor did
I feel satisfaction; I felt a combination of righteous moral justice
and deep sympathy for all the invisible and damaged boys in our
culture.

That doctor, I believe, was "Dave McConnell," formed and
shaped as a little boy into an evil man. While most of my empathy

will always go towards victims, I am glad I had enough empathy for the innocent boy in Dave and my doctor so that I could write his character effectively. Evil never begins in a vacuum. There is no more dangerous man than the one who has felt, for the many years of boyhood trauma, that he is powerless. This is why powerlessness sits at the heart of what goes wrong in males.

Although my molestation was not like Dave's—not severe enough to re-wire my brain to pedophilia—its trauma placed me in a tribe of millions of boys and girls who have been specifically targeted by brutal peers or dominant adults for dangerously inappropriate sexual contact. Like me, this global tribe of children fear life during adolescence, after our abusers tend to abandon us. Hopefully, as I did, they will seek therapy and support to heal. I became a mental health counselor professionally in part because I began therapy at sixteen and over the decades saw the gift of that profession. The human struggle to combat evil can take place as much in a therapy office as a battlefield, since all great human battles actually begin inside us. I won my struggle, but Dave McConnell did not win his.

In initial drafts of *The Stone Boys,* I wrote even more graphic scenes of sexual violence than you've read in this final book. Most of those brutal scenes were deleted for the sake of safe publication— especially so that school libraries, classrooms, and young adults could use the book. Even so, you may have found parts of the book disturbing, especially if you have read my other books, such as *The Wonder of Boys* or *The Wonder of Girls.*

"How can Gurian write these sexually graphic scenes?" you might wonder.

"Why would he even want to?"

"If he can write pedophiliac scenes, is he perhaps a perpetrator?"

If this book is used in literature and psychology classes in middle schools, high schools, and colleges, as I hope it will be, these questions could create powerful class discussion. I hope the following short answers will be of use. I have also created a Discussion section at the end of the book that I hope you'll use to start discussions in your classrooms, families, and other settings.

To the third and first questions: I am not a perpetrator, though I can imagine evil, just as Stephen King is not evil but can imagine pet cemeteries and demonic monsters, and Thomas Harris is not a cannibal but can imagine Hannibal Lector murdering and eating human flesh. Authors who imagine and depict evil have often experienced trauma in childhood and retained the trauma in imaginative work.

The human brain is an evolutionary masterpiece, always trying to heal itself. The wounds of the storyteller become gold if he or she is to survive and thrive in the world. Only when the wound stays hidden do we perish. All good art, I believe, is written, painted, and built by the wounded soul searching for its best self. Wounded artists write some of their work, as I have this book, first to tell a gripping story, but second, to help others heal.

As to the second question: I decided to retain some scenes of violence, e.g. at the lagoon, because the story absolutely need-ed them. Sexual trauma needs honesty—not gratuitousness, of course, but honesty. Nearly every day we hear in the news about another boy, girl, woman or man who has been sexually molested, harassed, abused, trafficked, or battered, yet a newspaper or social media post cannot fully tell the individual's story, especially be-cause sex is involved. A book, however, can move into the darker realms, and must do so.

For boys and men, this is true in what we in the psychology field call "a male-specific way." While all human beings live in a constant internal search for a self, males have fewer internal guideposts than females; young males take their adolescent and young adult risks in some part because they are trying to discover a reflected self in the world in which they take risks, perform, and grow. The normal confusion of being a boy in our new millennium is amplified tenfold when the boy is battered, from early on, by trauma perpetrated on him by other men.

Thank you for reading this book and letting its story enter your own internal field of vision. Whether *The Stone Boys* succeeds in schools and homes is your choice because it is you who makes the proper demands of the artist, and you who carries the power of human art to serve us.

Boys need us today in many of the same ways they have always needed us and in some new ways that we have barely begun to comprehend. At some point soon we will need to have a "Decade of the Boy" in which our civilization completely regroups to see what is happening to males all around us. Until then, I hope this small story has inspired you to discover two boys who are, like every boy around us, trying to make sense of it all as they strive to become good men.

—Michael Gurian, Spokane, 2019

# Q & A WITH MICHAEL GURIAN

**Q: Why did you write this book?**

**A: As a person in the psychological profession—a marriage and family counselor—I have long hypothesized that the moment we are aware of a traumatic experience in our own lives, we have the unconscious will to write it, color or paint it, express it in music or in woodworking or knitting or any craft or art.** Our brains, I think, are driven to bring the wound into the open, shape it, study it, judge it, put it away again, bring it back again, do war with it, make peace with it. We want to make the wound into gold. Instead of the wound driving us into despair in our lives, we all want, deep in our hearts, to turn it into motivation for growth.

So, I wrote this book for all these reasons:

* I had to write it, it lived in me, it had to come out.
* I felt a visceral need to tell the story of invisible American boys who are struggling to be good men in a culture that does not understand boys or men very well.
* Many of the books/characters I grew up with—Huck Finn/Tom Sawyer, Siddhartha/Govinda, *A Separate Peace*, *The Chosen*—involved two boys trying to care for one another, which is a sacred trust boys give and take, and I wanted to try to add two new American boys to the canon of literature in that vein.

* Being male and working for decades with male clients, I wanted to write a story that captures the difficulty of males expressing our tragedies and emotions in words—that difficulty makes for dramatic tension in a novel, and also for a deep catharsis when readers see the masks finally peeled off.

* After I had written many drafts of the book, I realized I wanted the book to be of service to children, adolescents, and adults who need to talk about personal experiences with trauma—bullying, sexual abuse, physical abuse. If the book touches some hearts and tongues enough to build conversation, it will go beyond my intention of writing a powerful story into, perhaps, saving a life.

* I wanted to write a young adult novel that could be used in any middle school, high school, or college as required or supplemental reading, to lead to discussions about all the subjects I just mentioned and a final one: the hidden world of boys that scares people because it is so often unexpressed but is, actually, a study in humanity striving to produce good *men*.

**Q: What age group ought to read this book?**

**A: Adolescents and adults.** I think some mature twelve-year-old readers will likely read it, but parental or teacher guidance ought to be required for that tender age. A fourteen-year-old or older should have the understanding to read it without issue, yet, because the book includes references to sexual content, including pedophilia, the book ought to be read with the intention of asking adults questions about what might be confusing. I hope adults will offer their assistance, even if the first time they do so they are rebuked by the child.

I have also written the book to be readable by nearly every reader of any reading level. One of our most pressing social issues today is the gradual loss of the love of reading among millions of our boys and young men. I hope even reluctant readers will read the book in order to find a piece of themselves in it, the piece I've referred to as universal: the internal male battle, visceral for all males, between good and evil.

**Q: Why is a lot of the book set on a Native American reservation, but you don't mention the name of the people or reservation?**

**A: My father had a contract like the one the book refers to on the Southern Ute Reservation during part of my teen years, so I am writing somewhat autobiographically.** While my parents were not divorced like Harvey and Judith, many other details are accurate to my boyhood, including Ben's work with his father during play rehearsals, and the use by the Southern Utes of the term "Rez."

All that said, out of respect for the Southern Utes and all indigenous tribes, I did not want to pretend I remembered everything perfectly from my teen years, and though I have done extensive research as an adult, I still felt it inappropriate to pretend I could completely and accurately appropriate or report sacred Southern Ute traditions and practices. As a white teenager, I was lucky enough to be befriended by some of the Southern Ute people, but I am not nor will ever be one of them. To protect their privacy and primacy of their traditions, I and my publisher decided a certain amount of anonymity was a good thing.

That said, I want to thank the Southern Ute people for letting me be involved with their traditions. When I took part in sweat lodge ceremonies as a teen in the 1970's, other people besides the Southern Utes were represented in the lodge, including Navaho and Hopi. Thus, I retained the reference to "Navaho" in Eagleclaw's words during the sweat lodge ceremony scene in the book. I want to thank all the tribes.

Since my teen years, I have participated in sweat lodge ceremonies with Lakota, Kalispell, Spokane, Nez Perce, and Northern Cheyenne tribe members. This has been an honor for me, and I consider the sweat lodge tradition to be one of the most sacred of rituals. The character of John Eagleclaw Simpson is in part based on a friend my father and our family had on the Southern Ute Reservation, and on other Native men who have affected my life positively.

**Q: Do you base your characters on a single person or are they usually an amalgam of people?**

**A: They are usually an amalgam of people and they are imagined in some mysterious way difficult to track in words.** Eagleclaw, I mentioned, was an amalgam, as were Harvey, Judith, Bert, Molly, Allen, Dave, and Ben. Ben, though my foil, is still an amalgam of other people as well as a product of imagination. Dave is also imagined, though some of the details of his character are amalgams of people I knew in my therapy practice.

I can't say I really know where characters and stories come from. Characters seem to form in my mind as seemingly whole people whom I give a name to in my notes right away so I can hold onto and develop them. I do long character sketches over time, but the initial "vision" of the character happens quite quickly in my head.

As these characters develop through action and scene and relationship, an illusion occurs: I begin to think, "Oh yes, I knew that person," as if my writing of the story gives the character a reality in my own past. But then, as I watch the character develop,

I realize I only knew a piece of this person. Much of the rest is imagined in service of the power, tension, and authenticity of the story.

**Q: What is your writing process? Is it part of your success as a writer?**

**A: I try to get up every morning and write for 2 to 4 hours.** I can't always do this, for instance if I am traveling to a school or conference and speaking there, but as much as possible, including weekends, this is my artistic and spiritual practice.

For many years, I taught writing at various universities where I was asked, "What makes you a writer?" I always answered, "That I write every day!" There are many ways to be a writer, and this is my way. I believe it is part of my success as a writer.

Success in any art form comes, I believe, from this kind of perseverance. While inspiration is important, the perspiration is equally important, if not more so. Writing every day is my way of capitalizing on both—if I'm writing, I'm ready for inspiration; and if I'm writing, I'm doing the perspiration part. This is two birds with one stone.

# Discussion Starters for

# Classrooms and Families

Do you remember any of the sexual abuse in this book happening to you, or anything like it? If so, don't say anything now in this class, but please come find me afterward so I can help you to tell me the story. Since there is no way you were or are at fault for what happened to you, there is no way I cannot love you through our conversations. I am here to help you in confidence. I will help you get the help you need.

1. What is shame? How is it different from guilt? Can you give examples from the book of both shame and guilt?

2. How did these two emotions drive Ben and Dave? Why is shame so paralyzing? Why does it keep us from telling the people we love what has happened to us? Should we allow it to do so?

3. What is a Fantasarian? Are there kids today who want to escape the world and become Fantasarians? In what ways are boys, in particular, doing this in your neighborhoods today?

4. Does the gold in the gold kitchen have any significance as a metaphor in this book? What other metaphors appear in the book and how are they significant?

5. What is the primary reason Ben smokes marijuana? Are there ways in which the people around you use something like marijuana—or marijuana itself—for some of the same reasons Ben did?

6. Did Dave become evil or is he just "sick?" When does a person "become" evil—is there an actual turning point when he or she is lost to the good?

7. Can people be born evil and/or is evil created by evil and traumatic acts perpetrated on children and adults?

8. Does the fact that Dave decided to get help from Ben show that he hasn't yet become evil or did he want Ben involved to test whether he was adept at evil manipulation?

9. Would Ben have participated with Dave in hurting Allen if he himself had not been sexually abused? If yes, why do you say that? If no, why?

10. Allen says, "I ain't no fag, and I ain't takin' my clothes off for no fags." Does he just use the word "fag" because that was a commonly used word in 1975 (and still today), or is it possible he also says what he says because of homophobia that is both culturally caused and personally caused by his abuse?

11. What do you think of Ben's and Dave's analysis of the difference between what kids and adults think should be done about a bully? In what way are both kids and adults right (and wrong)?

12. What is the significance of the sweat lodge in the novel, both as a place of pain and of healing and growth?

13. Is there significance to the novel taking place, in part, on a Native American reservation?

14. If so, what about this setting creates resonance for the dramatic center of the story?

15. What is the significance of the KKK costumes? How does that detail create levels of connection to other tragic and painful parts of human development?

16. How do boys become men? Does it just happen, or does it require certain activities and people to make it happen?

17. What is a man, in your opinion? Try using this tool—fill in the blank: "To me, a man is_____ _____." Here's an example I use in my books in psychology: A man is a loving, wise, and successful adult male.

18. Why did Ben's mother, Judith, tell Ben that talking about what happened—including the bad things Ben himself perpetrated—was the bravest thing a man could do?

# ACKNOWLEDGMENTS

The author wishes to acknowledge the great work of Jon Gosch, Brandon Krebs, Logan Amstadter, Susan Amstadter, Alan Rinzler, Russ Davis, and everyone else on the publishing and editing team who made this book a reality.

Over the last three decades I have had the privilege of speaking at almost a thousand schools around the country and abroad. I cannot put into words how much I appreciate the educators and the students at these schools. You've taught me much more than I've taught you, believe me.

Many friends and colleagues have helped me to express the emotional world of boys, including Michael Herzog, Ph.D., Pam Brown, M.A., Adie Goldberg, D.S.W., and Jeannie Corkill, M.S.W., all of whom provided psychological analysis, as well as sound literary advice. Many thanks also to Mic Hunter, specifically for his book, *Abused Boys*, and thank you to John Colson, Ph.D., Ross Coble, M.D., and Jeff Hedge, D.O., who answered difficult medical questions regarding the psycho-biology of molested boys.

My profound thanks to the people of the Southern Ute Reservation for their hospitality during my teen years, and thank you to Clayton Small of the Northern Cherokee for our times together in his sweat lodge during my adulthood.

Finally, and as always, thank you to my wife, Gail, and my daughters, Gabrielle and Davita, without whose loving support this novel would not have been written.